Runic Alphabet

For Włodek without whom the book would not
see the light of the day
For my parents Faina and Vilen Sonkin

Marina Sonkina

RunicAlphabet

And Other Stories

BOOKS

Edited by George Payerle
Cover design and artwork by Włodzimierz Milewski

Note for libraries: A catalogue record for this book is available from Library and Archives Canada at www.collectionscanada.gc.ca

ISBN: 978-0-9812476-0-1

Second Edition

BOOKS

MW Books
Garden Bay, BC
V0N 1S0
Canada
http://mwbookpublishing.com
info@mwbookpublishing.com

10 9 8 7 6 5 4 3 2

[signature]

RunicAlphabet

9

Christmas Tango

39

Carmelita

83

Bird's Milk

155

To Marjsha,
with gratitude.

[signature]

October 2010
Vancouver

Acknowledgements

I am enormously grateful to Włodzimierz Milewski who lovingly designed and produced the book. Special thanks to my insightful and patient editor George Payerle and my proofreader Kim Smith. I'm also forever indebted to my mother Faina Sonkina's unconditional love and editorial wisdom. My friends Allan MacInnis and Bruce Saunders gave their time and patience to the early drafts of the stories. And finally, I was the lucky beneficiary of Kent Harrington's friendship which gave me the courage to brave the waters of the English Language and inspired me in more ways than one.

Runic Alphabet

1

In the plant nursery, Witoslaw handed the money over to a girl behind the cash. Five minutes ago he didn't know he would be buying a tree.

The tree he had so unexpectedly acquired had a name attached to it on a white band clinging to its slender trunk. The Latin version he skipped, but the English he read with curiosity: "Japanese Snowbell." So far, the name meant little to him, except that the tree, like himself, was a foreigner, an exile in a new land.

In spite of its vulnerable look, it was already twice as tall as he. The most remarkable thing about it was the clusters of delicate white flowers that studded the branches from bottom to top. Permeated by the sun, the petals both retained and exuded light. If pure joy, yearning for some tangible form, could materialize out of thin air and move into the matter, it would choose this tree.

Though the tree was right in front of him, he couldn't quite convince himself that it wouldn't disappear – much like the face of an exquisite woman glimpsed by chance behind the window of a passing train. He had read somewhere that the Japanese have a special word for this fleeting, yet perfect love, when your fate presents itself in front of you in a flash, only to be dragged away along the tracks in smooth, hardly perceptible lurches, while you're still standing on the platform, spellbound, already fully aware that you will be yearning for this face for the rest of your life.

Witoslaw approached the tree and brought his squinting eyes close to its modest bell-shaped flowers. The petals gave off a delicate, tender fragrance. The aura of happiness and quiet exaltation enveloped him, as it always did in the presence of beauty.

Like beauty itself, the tree was mysterious: it stood there, silent, motionless, amidst varied but insignificant plants in plastic throw-away pots. It could not complain about the uncertainty of its future. All it did was filling his chest with accelerating and expanding palpitations. The more he looked at it, the more the world around him seemed to be changing coming into sharp focus as if viewed through special lenses that eliminated the fussiness of its outlines. Every speck of reality found its way directly into his mind, unfragmented, unbroken.

In that state of mind, scraps of conversation, people, street signs, a ribbed metal bottle cap on the pavement would stop drifting past his mind and fall effortlessly in their places forming a pattern the meaning of which would sooner or later be miraculously revealed to him.

Witoslaw knew that such states of sharpened consciousness were rare, and he yearned for them. Yet, out of superstition he hesitated to call these moments "inspiration," fearing to destroy that elusive butterfly by pinning it to the dull regularity of classification. But without that butterfly, his paintings would be nothing more than the sparkless renditions of a well-trained professional.

The artist touched the leaves of his tree: they were a miniature version of lilac. At the end of the sloping line, nature suddenly diverted from its rather overused oval, and took a smooth, but firm dip inward, then picked up on the forward thrust in order to finish the drawing with the light stroke of its pointed brush. A weak gust of wind sent a shiver through the branches: the leaves fluttered, infinitely responsive to air's every whim. The flowers on each branch looked like tiny parachutes ready to lift the whole tree up into the sky.

"I should put it into the ground right away," Witoslaw thought, picking up his new acquisition and loading it into his truck.

Back home he stood the tree in the middle of the lawn, in front of his house. Mentally, he drew a straight line from the tree trunk to the window of his studio.

"Right here ... That way I can see it all the time when I paint," he thought, figuring out where to dig.

He tried to balance the tree and was surprised at how heavily it weighed on his arm. His purchase came with a bundle of native soil now tightly swaddled in burlap and criss-crossed with ropes. This dry, stuck-together soil –

a sealed depository of vital juices, familiar bacteria and ferments – was the only thing connecting the tree with its past life. Like an anchor thrown overboard into alien waters, not reaching the bottom yet, it was now suspended in mid-fall.

The tag still attached to its trunk affirmed that the tree's life had been put on hold: a rough draft, an unanswered request for a place under the sun in this land of tough, red-necked, muscular cedars, firs and cypresses that shamelessly expanded upwards and downwards, grabbing the air, the earth, and the light, scattering their seeds ferociously around.

A gust of wind entangled itself in the tree's branches and it fell. Helpless, with half its flowers pinned under, it lay on its side, like a slain angel with wings crushed. Witoslaw rushed to its rescue. What he had to do was to restore its vertical line. Everything seemed to depend on that. Vertical meant life. Horizontal meant defeat, death, and decay. Even brought back to its normal position, the tree somehow looked helpless. Not an angel anymore, but a homeless orphan changing orphanages, always in transit with its meager belongings packed away in a grey sack huddled at its feet. Perhaps, it's the tag, thought Witoslaw, pulling a worn clasp knife from his pocket to remove the white band with its hardly-visible letters. Then he started digging.

"See, I found a home for you. Just be patient," he said

to the tree. "Soon I'll bury you, then you can start living for real ... isn't that strange? When they bury me, I'll be dust. But you'll grow roots, and then, perhaps, I'll grow roots too and won't look for another place." Witoslaw was making a pact with a tree: he promised it a home. It will be their new home, for both of them. "But you will have to take to this soil, to accept it. You agree?"

But the tree stood there silent, the wind gently picking at its branches.

2

The nursery's instructions were to dig a hole five times larger in diameter than the bundle of earth that the tree carried. This was a new, progressive method, they said, allowing the roots to spread horizontally with greater ease. The work seemed overwhelming. He would have to remove the sod, then replace it, after he finished the job. It would take a good portion of his morning, and the day would be lost for painting. By the time he finished, the special morning light he needed would be gone.

He looked at the spade he'd bought at a garage sale: the edge was dull. Making a deep enough hole would take ages, but he didn't have a file at hand. All he wanted was to get on with the job and finish it as soon as possible. Never having planted a tree before, he didn't feel any confidence in his hands. After all, this tree was a whim, he had no intention of becoming a gardener. He was simply struck by its fragile beauty and desired momentarily to possess it, a foolish bargain. He knew that the only way to possess something was to paint it.

Witoslaw was told in the nursery that the flowering lasted only three weeks. Somehow, in his mind, he stretched this number to an infinity, to a never-ending feast arranged for the pleasure of his eyes alone. He tried to cheer himself up. With the Japanese Snowbell right in front of the studio window, he would finally track down that ideal line permeating every form in the world, the line that so often eluded him.

And if the tree were to lose its flowers after he painted it, so be it. By the time that happened, the memory of that short-lived splendor would stay with him forever. He would learn to think fondly of the tree's subsequent plainness while waiting for the next spring.

He started to remove the sod. The ground beneath the black topsoil was a yellowish mixture of sand and rocks.

Soon the hole looked deep enough to completely cover the bundle of earth the tree had come with. But the labour of the five-times diameter remained. Witoslaw groaned and pressed on with his dull spade. When he finally stopped digging, he slumped onto the edge with his feet in the hole. It did look like a grave, maybe for a huge spilled dinosaur egg. After a while he emptied the sack of planting soil that he'd brought for good measure into the centre of his excavation, where the yolk would go, and mixed it well with sand. Then, firmly holding the tree down, he unfastened the ropes, removed the burlap and started filling the hole with earth.

At length, he stepped back: the vertical thrust was exact.

A short old man, all dried up and wrinkled, was gazing at the tree, squinting his eyes, his chin on the handle of a cane. God knows where he came from and how long he had been here.

"I just planted a tree," the artist said, unable to restrain his excitement. The man was silent.

"All I need is to water it and it's done. I hope it will live."

The old man continued to stare at the tree without saying a word. He cupped his ear, and quickly fluttered his fingers near his lips, in the gestural language of the deaf. Then he turned around and walked away.

3

During the next week the tree shed all its flowers. The first three days this looked like an innocent, if somewhat sly, game as if the beauty wanted to reach beyond its pre-scribed borders; as if it didn't matter for perfection where to manifest itself to the human eye: on the branches or down there on the earth. The fragrant snowflakes generously sprinkled the circle of black soil around the roots; the soil inside the circle looked like a minimalist painting.

On the fourth day, however, decay touched the flowers: they imploded and collapsed; a brownish mess cushioned the base of the tree. Black birds came to pick for worms in the exposed earth.

Every time Witoslaw had to pass by the tree, he averted his eyes. He felt that he had betrayed it. He had promised it a home but instead was killing it. Or perhaps it was the tree that had betrayed him by surrendering to decay.

Only in the evening, when the ultramarine shadows diluted the outline of the trunk and the branches, did thoughts of the Japanese Snowball ebb away. But at night, melancholy would take hold of the artist. He imagined the choked cry of the roots searching blindly in the earth. What exactly the roots were looking for at night – water, a particular combination of minerals that give them life – he didn't know. Those voiceless cries, suppressed by the weight of the soil, tormented him no less.

On one such night, after staring into the eyes of insomnia for several hours, Witoslaw decided to get out of bed. He couldn't find his bath-robe but didn't want to wake up his mistress by looking for it in the dark. He walked over to his studio, naked, shivering from the night breeze. Boxes still unpacked after the move into this house cast diffused rectangular shadows on the floor. His unfinished canvasses were stacked facing the wall. I might as well empty some boxes, he thought, giving up any hope of sleep. In the dark, the coarse sound of the tape torn off the cardboard was brutal, like sudden pain.

His eyelids were heavy with fatigue, yet he didn't turn on the light, relying instead on one street lamp for a complete redecoration of his studio. The fugitive light from outside the window turned the newspapers scattered on the floor into feeble beacons that guided his eyes through the labyrinths of frames, boxes, canvasses, and the white papier-mâché cubes and spheres that he used for his still lifes. The chairs were grotesque monsters wrestling with each other in the centre of the room, some mounted on the backs of others, their legs up.

His Japanese Snowbell had also changed. Its trunk laid a dark shadow across the window pane.

Without looking, Witoslaw submerged his hands into the first box that came his way: albums, mixed up with old postcards and books and more albums – he had to find homes for all these vagabonds forced under the same roof by moving. Right now, in the stillness of the night, the task seemed enormous, beyond his reservoirs of energy.

He fumbled through papers, ready to give up, when at the very bottom of the box his fingers stumbled onto something cold and metallic. He jerked his hand away as if he had grabbed an electric wire, but one second was enough to shake the remnants of night-stupor from him. He recognized an ornate handle on the lid of a small chest.

Inside it were Ariadna's letters. There were also tapes with recordings of her voice, a black and white photograph of her face, a slim volume of Italian poetry she had given him, and some other trinkets that would mean nothing to the outside world, had the world by some fluke suddenly brought them into broad daylight. He shuddered at the thought of their imagined exposure, though he knew perfectly well that the world didn't care.

He had packed these possessions according to a hierarchy known only to his heart.

Ariadna's photograph, his most cherished treasure, was at the bottom, safely tucked under the velvet lining of the chest: the photo had to be separate from the letters and tapes piled up on top of it.

When packing it, he tried not to leave any spaces unfilled (he always pretended to himself that his box was more crammed full than it really was) and inserted in each corner small rolls of sketches that he had made of Ariadna on their last day together. On top he put numerous drawings that he later made of her from memory.

Sitting on the floor, with the box weighing coldly in his listless arms, he tried to regain his breath, watching his everyday life closing over his head. It was always the same, every time he touched what was left of her – a quick spasm in his throat, then obscurity, darkness, objects around him losing all their meaning and purpose, their contours becoming more impenetrable, more enigmatic than usual. One might look at a vase, or a wall and ask: "What is it?" or "Why is it here?" and find not a hint of an answer in one's own memory.

He felt like a buffoon from a fairy-tale of his childhood who had accidentally crossed some forbidden line and was now being punished with impending death. And while he lay there prostrated, awaiting the worst, some fairy turned up with a bucket of magic "death" water and sprinkled him from head to toes – to let him die fully and irrevocably. But once he was filled to the brim with his own death, the fairy would empty a handy bucket of "life" water on his body and he would jump to his feet, feeling fresh springy life in every muscle.

"Death" water first, then "life", then – the resurrection. Only many years later, when all that was left of her were his memories and these faded letters now obscurely glimmering in the dark, did he understand the meaning of this strange baptism.

There were no witnesses to his transformation except the tree behind the dark window pane and its shadow on the floor. At night the tree continued to shed its flowers, caught up like himself between death and life.

Ariadna knew nothing about this tree, as for so many years now, she had known nothing about his life. She knew nothing about his wanderings, his doubts, his spasms of wintry immobility when he couldn't so much as keep a brush in his hand, overwhelmed by a sudden fear. So many things had happened without her: the map of the world had been refashioned; old walls had been destroyed, new ones erected; he had given up the brilliant colours he was famous for as a young man, in favour of a translucent milky, silvery palette. He had now moved to another city, another continent, and had a new lover, the "newest" one.

4

There were moments when his life, he thought, was still an open book for Ariadna. She continued to read it with rapture in her death the way she had always read it when she was alive. Somehow, even after her death almost twenty years ago, she kept the protective wings of her soul over him. There were moments when he didn't doubt it. Then there were darker days of insipid conviction that she had abandoned him forever. On such days it seemed to Witoslaw that she knew nothing of a long and convoluted chain of events whose meaning so often eluded him too. Yet he wanted to hope, against all odds, that what was hidden from him would somehow become transparent to her on the account of her unusual, if precarious, status: being dead for the world, yet alive for him. He even believed that her knowledge, miraculously intimated to him, would somehow ultimately save him ...

It cannot be that she doesn't know how I, after the news of her death, have also succumbed to stupor. But I, being the only guardian of all our moments together (58 hours, 42 minutes, I once counted), the only keeper of the quiet radiance of her face, the only one who knows how all of her – the gentle slope of her shoulders and the mole under her chin – assumed this melancholic quality, when she was leaning over the book – I, being the only witness, couldn't afford dying together with her, and had to drag along my guts and my heart that never stopped sobbing for her, never stopped sobbing.

5

Immediately after her death, he felt a desperate urge to contact her husband, and ask him for one exceptionally generous gesture: could he not perhaps give him something that was left of her? It didn't matter what: her childhood photographs, or even that dark blue dress she was wearing the last time he saw her. He couldn't have thrown it away, that would be unthinkable. I will not abuse your hospitality, I'll just pick up whatever you can give – and disappear.

With time the hand of insanity loosened its grip, and

Witoslaw found himself standing alone on the crust of the earth observing clouds and kingdoms passing by, while she was hidden inside, deep in the black soil.

Now she descends into the earth, now she is on a level with telephone cables, electrical wires, dead water pipes and pure water pipes, now she descends to deeper places, deeper than deep, there lie the reason for all this flowing, now she is in the layers of stone and ground water, there lie the motives of war and the movers of history and the future destines of nations and people." The lines came to him from somewhere but he couldn't remember who it was ...

Silently Ariadna and Witoslaw were whirling round and round, each in their dwelling on the same earth. The tectonic plates were shifting, rubbing at each other's shoulders, pushing out hot lava and pumice, and they were far apart. But sometimes – today was such an occasion – they would meet in the darkness of the night, inside an ornate chest sitting now on his lap.

The desire to look at her face overpowered him. The photo was his last resort, kept for the emergency cases: days of despair when his brush would fail him, or when he was packing his suitcase up before visiting his daughter in yet another city.

Usually, Witoslaw was unwilling to superimpose the anguish of his own life over the pure line of her forehead which, for so many years now, was unfailingly leaning towards his soul. As if he was afraid that the photograph's powers would diminish, from too frequent a contact with this world. But today was a different day. His tree was shedding flowers – it was dying. He was trespassing the promise he gave it, and he needed Ariadna's help.

Contemplation of her face always filled him with great tenderness; it melted all the harshness this world imparted onto him. He was ready to forgive himself for aging so rapidly, for producing such mediocre art, for continuing to live after she was dead. Her eyes, quiet and grey, with a distinct darker rim around the pupil, dispensed mercy that fortified him and brought him back to the mysterious source of his life where everything became possible, fully transparent and pliable.

He didn't need any props to remember how her dark chestnut hair fell in a straight cascade over one cheek – as if some invisible breeze was still stroking her face – leaving the other one exposed to the very temple, and further down to the lobe of her ear. The smallness and vulnerability of that ear never failed to move him. Somehow he imagined that her gentleness started there – inside that little shell – and then spread over her face, her hands, her arms, her whole body, spilling over into the world. Every time he looked at her face the world became inhabitable again.

He found it handy to keep a little dictaphone inside the chest. He pressed a button without turning on the light, and her warm low voice stepped into the room in the middle of a phrase: he must have forgotten to rewind the tape the last time he listened to it.

It is night here. I'm almost asleep, but in your city it must be morning already, and you're wide awake ... How strange time is ...

He was both elated and becalmed by the rich modulations of her voice. It was uncanny; she was long dead, yet so close, so alive, hiding somewhere in the mechanics of the talking box. She had a strange manner of gliding off the vowels at the end of words, as if she was tired, or simply knew the excessive effort was unnecessary when talking to him: as if both of them could do without words.

Often she would read him poetry, most of it by heart.
Look how lightly the dragonflies
Carry a rainbow on their wings.

She would pause trying to remember the next line.
Without dropping it into the pond
Full of water lilies.

Witoslaw loved those moments of hesitation. They gave him a more direct access to the life of her soul than words themselves. When she read from the book, he would hear the rustle of pages under her fingers as she whispered: "No, that's not it, and this is not that," trying to find something she imagined he would like. The illusion of seeing her eyes moving along the page made him suffer again.

There was silence on the tape, interrupted only by her breath. He became aware that he was still alone in his studio, naked in the middle of the night, clad only in his aging, greyish flesh. He shivered.

On one occasion she must have forgotten to turn off the tape-recorder at the end of a poem and he heard the rough sound of the chair being pushed back, then some muted clattering, and then water running, pots clanging. She must have started cooking, unaware of her uninvited visitor, forever listening to her, frozen in the corner of her invisible kitchen. What meal was she preparing in that moment, now twenty years ago? Who would have gathered around her table? These acoustic fossils, these leftovers of her life accidentally immortalized by a primitive machine, became a no-man's land that he greedily appropriated while she herself was gone, leaving him with the sounds of bygone pots and pans.

"I want to spend every waking moment with you," he once said to her on the phone. "Describe to me things you see right now. The street you're walking on, trees, people."

Ten days later, on another tape, she took him for a walk.

"See that trolley with horses? It's a hot day here, the end of the holidays, lots of tourists, gaudy crowds, twin girls with balloons just passing by ... One has the red one, and the other – yellow."

Her voice was fading, gradually taken over by the noise of passing cars, the remote jingle of a bell from the trolley with horses. Soon it re-emerged:

"See an old lady dressed in frills. She is pushing a supermarket cart with two ducks, also in frilled caps, and aprons, and pink ribbons. I often see her in this park ... I think she is a fortune teller. I should ask her next time to tell me what will happen to us ... I cannot breathe without you much longer, I can't ... "

Her voice was now bare thread; she couldn't talk for a while. But he continued to walk by her side, through this silence. He didn't want her to cry: her tears would have torn his heart. She must have read his mind and forced her tears back.

"Now we are coming closer to where I live," she said in a lifeless voice.

"Do you see those tall trees? Right there! Two monkey puzzles, H-m-m ... I always thought them ugly ... Let me move into the shade here, away from the crowds. That's better, now I can talk to you. Can your hear me, my love?"

Her voice came back to life again: "Oh, look at these red-breasted robins! They flit from bush to bush, peck at some berries ... what do you call this bush? Sycamore?"

Again there was a pause, and he could hear cars passing by, children shouting, and some far-away whistle. "Now lift your head. See this clown high up in the sky? He has a hat with a pompon, one pant leg is striped, and then below, I think, are his feet in huge white shoes. Oh, look, the right shoe is melting away ... Now the leg is disappearing. ... Do you see it? I wonder what are you looking at in this moment in your snowy city? I'm looking at the clouds but I can turn around and I see you, standing behind my shoulder."

6

Witoslaw stopped the tape-recorder. In the silence of the night, he heard the uneven beats of his heart. He knew that in a moment the clown would turn into a monster with fuzzy sleeves dispensing torrents of rain. And she would be running away from the rain, and he next to her, forever bound to the sound of her breath and water pouring down her face, her chest, her hair; and she would forever be looking for a shelter for both of them in that park with the monkey puzzle trees, as she was turning left or right, towards a big cedar. He would have no say in her itinerary, trying to keep up with her again and again for the last twenty years along the imagined route preserved by this tape. All he could do was follow her, breath to breath, shoulder to shoulder, getting soaked in a rain that hadn't ceased for twenty years. He couldn't stop it, no more than he could stop her from dying.

If he could, he would have sheltered her, saved her,

found the way for them to be together while she was still alive. Fate plucked two of them out of a million, put invisible tags around their wrists so that they could stand out in the crowd and be seen anywhere they went. Then the same fate smuggled them from each other to different continents, jailed then into small impenetrable cells, chaining her to her husband, him to his then wife.

In their naiveté or arrogance, they tried to cheat their destiny. They kept plotting and scheming, picking cities on the map in which to meet, however fleetingly. But the chosen dates collided with unforeseen obstacles in their other lives;   weeks collided with weeks, months, then exploded, and died. Hotels and pensions they planned on staying in, dodged them leaving nothing but the echo of their names.

Then, in desperation, as their last resort, they found this little machine. It could swallow thousands of miles without blinking, simulate reality and raise the temperature of their longing for each other tenfold. Finally they realized the only place they could stage their lofty, tender and forlorn trysts was in the metal intestines of a plastic box.

Witoslaw listened to her voice, and peace came to his soul, grief melted into joy and he didn't know the difference between the two anymore – where grief ended and joy began. Nor did it matter.

The morning came and pain didn't exist, nor death, nor remorse, nor self-pity. What did it: her voice talking to him again, her face? All he knew he was free: sore in his heart, tired, but free.

7

On the floor he noticed two dry ginkgo leaves, pale in the uncertainty of a bleak morning. They must have fallen out of her letter while he was scrounging for her photograph.

On the day when Witoslaw and Ariadna had to part, she went to the park near the station from which his train had just pulled off. There she sank under a tree, as she wrote later in her letter, into a state of oblivion. When, finally, she came to her senses, she found herself sprawled on a bright carpet of small, unusually shaped yellow leaves. These were two-lobed, simple triangles with the sides only slightly curving away from the straight line. There was something rudimentary, even primordial about their shape. Held by a stem upside down, they could pass for an Indian tepee, she wrote him. But if you flipped them back, they turned into the tiny fan of a fairy ... Or perhaps, it was a shard of some Runic alphabet, just one surviving vowel, a muttered litany of never-ending a-a-a-a.

These were ginkgo leaves, a "blueprint, a rehearsal of God's future craftsmanship" as she put it. Another name for it was *Ginkgo Biloba*, or Maiden Hair. "If you bring the leaf, this little fairy's fan, against the light, instead

31

of the usual net of convoluted green veins running in all directions, you will see a membrane as smooth and polished as the perfectly combed hair of a young woman." Maiden Hair had survived dinosaurs and the Ice Age, remaining unchanged for 260 million years. But then the Creator, as if embarrassed by his first crude attempts, must have perfected his skills and come up with more refined and intricate patterns: oak leaves, maple leaves, tulip tree leaves. Japanese Snowbell ... God then swept the original prototype under the carpet of the remote provinces in Southern China where, millions of years later, the Buddhist monks found it. They believed in the sacred powers of ginkgo: it could cure a melancholic heart and return a lost love ...

Witoslaw carefully put the fragile leaves back into the envelope.

He didn't notice how the room started to come to its senses in the grey milk of dawn. As in a developing negative, objects appeared one by one, first in an outline, then in flesh: canvasses, wrestling chairs, a chest turned inside out, the letters, the tapes, the tape-recorder, the rolls of drawing scattered around him.

Soon not a trace of night was left. The day was standing there erect and plain-faced, all up for grabs, as crude as the deeds it would be filled with. Unlike the night, that belonged to him, the day was everybody's fleamarket.

He looked out onto the street. Separated from him

only by a windowpane, his Japanese Snowbell was like an unfinished painting in the morning mist.

He suddenly understood what he was looking at. The tree was Ariadna herself, that part of her that had never died, but continued to live all these years without revealing itself. In that tree, in the ephemeral beauty of its bloom, she had finally found the home that for so many years eluded her.

Her previous attempts to find form for herself had all failed – he was witness to that. One late afternoon he saw a familiar silhouette crossing a bridge; the same dark brown hair flying in the wind, the same small stride. It took him running half-way across the bridge to catch her up, but then he saw Ariadna's awkward scheming: the woman was old, with a heavy jaw and muddy eyes.

His beloved hadn't turned into a tree the way nymphs in sun-drenched ancient groves had: shrieks and heavy panting, eyes coming out of their orbits and near surrender to the lustful arms of gods at the end of a messy chase. No, she had prepared him for her metamorphosis long ago: having sent him two leaves, now dry, a message written in a lost Runic script, she now entered the tree calmly as familiar essence enters familiar essence, blood enters blood, water enters water, beauty enters beauty.

He could see her now beyond the window, separated from him and his easel only by the sheet of glass. She was standing there waiting. Once again she had moored to his heart, uncertain of herself, with a bundle of earth as her only possession.

He couldn't betray her a second time, by letting her die again. This time she would live ... Promise me you will live. Promise me this time, for I won't, I can't survive your death all over again.

Later in the day, he returned to the nursery. He recognized the girl who had sold him the tree:

"My tree is dying," he said. "I bought it from you three weeks ago."

"What tree was that?"

"Japanese Snowbell. Do you remember I bought it?"

"No, not really. We have lots of customers ... "

"I must have a receipt somewhere."

"Is it really that bad?"

"By the look of it. It's dropping all its flowers."

"It may be in shock. But if it dies, you have a warranty for a year. You can bring it back and be reimbursed."

"I don't want to bring it back. I want it to live."

"Try to water it well. It needs good drainage. Wait till next year and see what happens."

Back home, Witoslaw poured some water into the dark circle around the tree. In its thirst the earth greedily sucked up two buckets. It gave him pleasure to imagine roots absorbing water through hundreds of capillaries and then redirecting it to the trunk, and from the trunk to each branch, and from each branch to leaves and flowers.

He gently rubbed a leaf between his index and big finger, checking it for resilience. It was flaccid. Was it so tender because of its nature, or was it slowly and imperceptibly succumbing to death? It was hard to say. "Of course you're in shock. When you accept a new soul into you, you're always in shock. New soul going into new soil. Drink, we'll somehow manage together. You have your own home now, not just a tape-recorder inside a box or memories inside my heart for I too will go one day ... Drink. You are free now. We are both free. Like in that poem you read to me once, remember?"

She is free. Free from the body.

And free from the soul and from the blood that is the soul,

Free from wishes and sudden fear

And from fear for me, free from honour and from shame

Free from hope and from despair and from fire and from water,

Free from the colour of her eyes and from the colour of her hair,

Free from the furniture and free from knife, spoon fork,

Free from round seals

And from square seals

Free from photos and free from clips,

She is free.

The dying cinders of sunset were pouring over the top of the Japanese Snowbell. High above his head, clouds with a crimson lining were blowing soundlessly their high-order sails, drifting away into some unknown land. He turned around and saw Ariadna standing behind his shoulder.

Another flower, a perfectly chiselled tiny bell, detached itself from her branch and parachuted pensively to his feet. It was crimson in the rays of the setting sun.

To R.L.

Christmas Tango

1

"That hole I'm living in, man! I'm glad I'm out of there," he bellowed in my face, and gulped down his third beer.

Hunched on a stool, feet dangling, the man was short, stout and sloppily dressed in worn-out corduroys, his shirt unbuttoned down to his fat belly. He smelled.

"Fucking holes, with no fucking *milongas*. Women who haven't got a clue how to walk, never mind dance. I've had it!"

I had no interest in arguing with him. Tango or no tango, wrong city or right, I really didn't care.

"Another beer," the short man said, tossing some coins on the counter.

He slurred, his vowels riding over a bumpy road strewn with hurdles in the most unexpected places. I knew he was loaded. Without looking at him, I knew. I felt his back was swaying, while all the time he tried to keep it ramrod straight.

I didn't say anything. He slid off his stool and moved closer, making an attempt to put his arm around me to prop himself up, but I was much taller than him, so he missed the target, staggered, and went high for my baseball cap instead. His hand dropped to half-mast while he tried to pull the peak over my eyes, as if I was still a kid.

"Watch it, pal," I said just in case, my voice drowning in the racket of three television sets suspended over the heads of the drinkers. The *Montreal Canadiennes* scored.

"Don't you look at me as if you just snuffed somebody," he said with a sudden influx of energy. "When you feel like blasting the whole world, you go and you tango, get it? You're a lucky son-of-a-bitch. In this city you can do tango Monday, Tuesday, Wednesday, every night you go tango and to hell with it all. Where I live, there is no fucking tango, and I come here and what am I doing? Trying to find that sneaky bitch instead of going to *milonga*! Come on, let's go to Lilly. What, you don't know Lilly on St. Laurent? Oh, man!" He started laughing.

"You better keep away from Lilly, then! Gorgeous woman! Not for brats like you, though! She'll gobble you up! Ha-Ha-ha! Know where Lilly is? Corner of St. Bernard. Next to that place, what's it called?" His fingers came together in a soundless click: "Where they used to cut gravestones. Ah, never mind! On Tuesday you go to Tangueria, on Thursday there is *milonga* at Geraldo's. Don't go to Juan, though. Juan is full of shit, he gives you all this nonsense about the steps till you drop dead. Forget it! Tango is not in the steps. It's in your fucking soul." He swayed away from me.

"Bartender, another beer for me and my young friend," he called to the red-lipped blonde behind the bar, trying to wave a hand and stay vertical at the same time.

"I have to go now," I said.

"Have to go ... He has to go! And what about me? Where do I go? My best friend screwed me. Took fifty grand and buggered off with my wife ... I came home – no wife, no money, no furniture, no nothing ... But anyway, that's not the point. Forget about it, let's drink. "

This man was pissing me off.

"You listen to me. I gonna tell you something that nobody will tell you. You'll be grateful to old Shorty."

Yeah, Shorty, I thought, you're tanked all right.

"If you come and the fucker puts you to the barre, and makes you practice with the barre, instead of a woman, that's how you know he is a fucking bullshitter. You practice your *sacadas* and *boleos* with a woman, not with the barre. The barre is dead, it doesn't breathe. You go for the thing that breathes. You get it?"

"Yes, I get it," I said and handed my money to the bartender. I got off the stool and headed for the exit. I'd had enough of him. I knew nothing about tango, and had no intention of looking for a tango teacher. I had my own life to live, and he was dragging me into his personal problems and his tango crap. Even through his drunkenness, which often smoothes the edges out in people, I could sense some sharp, angular madness in him. His obsession running like an idling engine, all on its own. He jumped off the stool in an unexpectedly quick, midget-like movement, trying to prevent me from leaving.

"Come on, have another drink, it's on me." He was now facing me, waving his arms in the air, and then holding them up in front of himself, as if embracing an invisible partner. "I'm telling you it's all in the embrace, it's the energy, it's not the steps. Everybody thinks they learn the steps and that's the dance! Nonsense! It's how you breathe and how you hold a woman."

He moved closer to me. I instinctively stepped back. He disgusted me.

"If you hold her right, she will give you everything she has. If she is a good dancer, she knows how to surrender herself. She will be pouring herself into you!"

He shifted ground to whisper. "All you have to do is to take her and lead her wherever you please. You're in control, and if you're any good, she'll let you have it. Never ask for her name or anything. Her life is her business, that's the magic of it ... Where else can you get it? This is better than sex, I'm telling you."

The puck went into the goal again, and his rumblings sank beneath the cheers of the customers. But I'd heard him, and what I heard tantalized me. Could it really be so easy to get close to a woman? I couldn't even remember when I last had a woman. It must have been years.

I didn't say anything to Shorty, but felt a sudden pity for myself. It descended right to my stomach, making it feel hollow and tight. I suddenly became agreeable and limp, as if all the air had been knocked out of me. Shorty prodded me back onto a stool and ordered another round.

Though I'm almost thirty, I'm still shy with women. I'm not particularly good-looking, you see. My lanky frame does not put its height to any good use. I stoop and walk in long uneven strides, with a slight jerk at the end of each step, an unconscious attempt to make the difference in my shoulders' height less conspicuous. My adolescent bones couldn't cope with rapid growth, you see, and I developed scoliosis, overlooked by my absent-minded aunt.

In my whole life I never managed to figure out what to do with my arms: they dangle along my body without any purpose. But there's nothing wrong with my face. You can't say anything against my face. I'm not particularly handsome, true, but I am not unattractive either. My eyes, for example. You'd always want to look at them again. Out of curiosity. It's their color, mostly: washed out blue, almost white but with a dark rim around the pupil, unusual for a man. Redheads and albinos have such eyes, but I have a mass of dark hair on my head, and a shy little smile that doesn't expose my teeth. Lately, I've been trying to grow a small moustache.

Even though my features are not irregular, they must harbour some warp, an intangible swerve, a deeply hidden deformation that more than anything else may explain why it's so difficult for me to meet ladies. Women intuitively feel that I align myself with some asymmetry lurching out of every corner if you want to really look. They find it disturbing. Women like a straight line. And where can I get that line with my constant self-doubts, empty pockets and a hole in my sock?

One girl – nice legs, otherwise nothing special – burst into tears at that very moment when normal women are supposed to melt into blissful fatigue; anyhow, this girl sobbed into my ear: "You hate me, because you hate yourself!" Where did you get all this pop psychology crap, I wanted to ask her, but didn't. Because women don't hear you anyway. And why would I hate her? I didn't care one way or another … But later I thought, she might've hit onto something here! You dislike others as long as you dislike yourself. Ha! That's a thought! That sort of makes sense to me, come to think of it! By the way, I never claimed I liked myself. As for other people, what's there to like? Well, women, maybe. Maybe. Only if you know how to handle them.

What I mean is that women expect a man to know "what he wants, and where he's going," as they say in sitcoms.

How can I know what I want? Every minute I'm pulled in opposite directions. To go for one thing means to deny myself another. And if I deny myself that other wish, I'm only half fulfilled, while the other half of my confused, contradictory self remains forever needy and orphaned!

For some men all it takes is to narrow their eyes just

so, and say nothing; stand and sway lightly on their heels, hands in their pockets. That's it! Say nothing at all, don't even smile, just squint your eyes like so, and she's done, she's cooked. Deep down, every woman wants to give herself up, to surrender completely, body and soul. "Just take me, lift all the responsibility off my shoulders, and I'll be yours." Scary business!

What spoils the game for me is that I always give away my eagerness. Too much yearning in my eyes, too much *I'd give anything to have you* ... True, I sometimes manage to put a stern mask of indifference on my face, and then there is no way out of it, except rubbing my mask against theirs – a dance many of them are so good at.

And yet, if only you knew how I saw you – you stern secretaries, you tight-lipped accountants, short-skirted administrators! – I see you as enigmatic sirens, bred by the high tide of the sea, beautiful, serene and enticing! You're holding wreaths of glory in your marble arms, and sing the songs that make the earth whirl around Why don't you sirens ever scribble me your phone number on a scrap of paper under the dim light of a street lamp, fumbling in your handbags? Sorry, no pen, will a piece of lipstick do?

Of course, it will! I accept telephone numbers written in blood.

2

On windy December nights the world is aloof and unyielding. Rare passersby in the street, brooding lonely ghosts. You can't approach them and strike up a conversation. They'll cross over to the other side of the road before you get close.

I have only one tool for probing this hostile world – the joyful and persistent alertness of my private parts. While I myself, in my absent-mindedness, can overlook things, my privates react instantaneously to minute changes in the brightness of the world's feminine filament, standing to full attention at the sight of any skirt swaying by; feeling the mute, dark necessity for action even in the presence of a long-legged, vapid bill-board girl sporting a modest bikini. At the same time, the most far-fetched congruity of images can subsume my tool's primitive power into sublime bliss.

Last year, in a rare moment of peace, I got beside a small pond of lilies in a city park. It was early spring and the sight of the lilies, the exquisite purity of their half-closed curves, suddenly catapulted my hair-trigger instrument into a state of euphoria. After that, how could I underestimate this crude tool that could so easily, in a blink of my own eye, elevate me to such metaphysical heights? It has been alerting me to the state of world affairs since I was six. After all, this possession of mine is the only thing that makes me real in the phony world and makes the phony world real for me.

After I met Shorty in the bar, one thought kept rankling me: what do men do with their tool of cognition under certain circumstances? Or, to put it bluntly, how can they avoid a hard-on while dancing tango? Do they get so used to women that they stop feeling any excitement and become completely desensitized?

One Sunday night, when I had nothing much to do, and nobody to call, I decided to satisfy my curiosity and take a tango lesson. Who knows? Who might I meet there?

But it was the middle of the month, and no studios accepted drop-ins. I had to pay cash for the rest of the course, seven or eight classes.

I took my grandfather's old chronometer that was collecting cobwebs in the corner of my room into the antiquarian marine shop. The two hundred bucks that I got in return solved the problem.

I discovered quickly that Shorty had lied to me about tango. Indeed, tango *was* in the steps: in the endless repetition of the basic steps and turns. But the clean, precise, sharp yet unhurried footwork combined with the leisurely nonchalant attitude ("I may turn when it pleases me or not turn at all") was completely beyond my reach. Yet, difficult as they seemed, turns were easier to execute than tango walking. "Walk like you breathe, tranquillo, tranquillo," commanded Alfredo, a dark Argentinean in black soft velvety pants and a massive golden chain showing through the open collar of his loose silk shirt.

"It's easy," he said. Thrusting back his gelled pitch-black hair, he walked with the confidence of a commando, and the regal sleekness of a cat. He firmly, but gently, probed the floor with the tip of his arching foot, caressing it ever so lightly, and then thrust his hips forward, while his torso was still slightly tilted back. Never, never could I learn to walk like that!

There were twice as many women in the class as men, and I had to dance with each of them to be fair to all. In tango jargon, women are called "followers" and men "leaders". Most of the "followers" were plain-looking, rather tired middle-aged ladies who had summed up youthful buoyancy for the occasion; only two women were in their twenties, and of those two one was pregnant. Like me, these women were struggling with their steps. Awkward and gravity-bound, they sheepishly trod the floor, as if stepping into a capsizing boat. They jolted in the most unexpected places; or came to a sudden halt, abandoning the music completely.

But I had an even harder time with the whole thing than these women. While "followers" at least could focus on their steps, I had to choreograph those steps for them, all the time paying close attention to the music; I had to watch out for other couples, and navigate the floor, always counter-clockwise. Leading turned out to be tricky and I sweated profusely. Besides, how do you silently communicate to a woman what you intend to do next?

"With your whole body, not just your arm," explained Alfredo.

"Hold her light, but firm, Chasen!" That's how he pronounced my name. "Where your hand, where your body? The arm on her back, the body went out for lunch. They together, your body and arm, no?"

"They should be," I conceded.

"Put your hand over there," he pressed my listless hand against my partner's back. "Strong, but easy, don't push her; she feel your power through your chest. From the waist up you one creature. Make senses, no? – Make senses," he answered for me, as was his habit.

"Move closer to her, no fear. She's a woman, you're a man, no? She won't eat you. Ladies? Leave your head home, ladies! I don't want your head. I want your body! This is tango! In Buenos Aires we dance close embrace, you better get used to it now. Men, ankles together, ladies, knees together. Don't look at your feet, close your eyes, ladies, feel the man. You don't feel him, he don't lead; no lead, no dance. It's not your husband, don't boss your man here! And we go now. One, two, three, four, five, six, seven, eight! Now, the music!"

My only saving grace was my sense of rhythm. I had

come to love tango music and gradually it entered my blood stream. It took me five months of steady practice to learn to walk. And then it came to me! It happened to me, it entered my core: together with music, I cried for the world, I wept, I melted with sorrow. Tango both humbled and raised me out of the ashes, all in a single note, sighed out by a *bandoneoni*. Sometimes fear would overcome me again, and I'd become uncertain of my steps; then I would breathe the air of movement and hope, right through my core, through the center – no, not through the lungs, through the diaphragm, as Alfredo used to say. And the greatness of tango filled my heart, loosened my legs.

I walked to the sad and solemn sounds of the *Cumparsita*. I was that soul in the masquerade, a soul waiting at a wharf in an alien port while the foreign ships, ablaze with garlands of light, came and sailed away, and left me waiting.

"La comparsa de miseries/ sin fin desfila/ en torno de aquel ser enfermo/ que pronto ha de morir de pena." [1]

I now felt the addiction of tango. It was like life itself: repetitive, yet always new, full of unforeseen trickery, archness and drama; it teased me with rich promises that were immediately taken away, and bestowed upon me sudden, unexpected blessings. Like life, it had a powerful undercurrent, an all-penetrating pulse that could drown

---

1 *A masquerade of miseries/ marches endlessly around me./ Soon,/ I too will die of pain. (Translated by the author)*

you if you were not attuned to it. You had to dissolve yourself in tango, in music, and let the music carry you to the place of your greatest fear and sadness, and take you out of it and bring you back, while you had to take its dark throbbing into your very veins, and look into the abyss it was leading you to. You were naked in tango, you couldn't hide, no more than one can hide from life. You had to trust tango as a new-born baby trusts life. You had to be exuberant, cruel but gentle, while the music was still playing. You had to draw the knife at the sight of treachery but then pause and tuck it away and turn around and forgive, forgive that woman.

And sometimes, in moments of confusion, you had to stop moving and absorb the stillness; for there was a pause in the trajectory of the flight.

I discovered that there were women who knew the steps and danced well; but then there were others whose knowledge of the technique was deeply buried inside them; they could stop and do nothing at all or take the risk and accompany you on a perilous journey because they trusted you. They had an uncanny knowledge of how you were in the world and how you breathed; they intuited your next step and moved together with you effortlessly, with a certain languished passivity, as if they had no will of their own; they did not devour your freedom; they just followed you along the undulations of the music; these women were the very best dancers and most in demand.

A long time ago I'd passed the point of no return. To pay for more and more classes, I sold antique jewellery my mother left me. I moved into an even smaller flat further east, and supported myself on some odd jobs during the day while continuing to dance at night.

Yet at the beginning tango didn't make my life easier. The contrast between the times spent in the studio and the drawn-out hours I wasted in the hole I could never call home made my solitude even more unbearable.

I remember one occasion especially, when I stepped into the night, after practicing tango, and saw the stars over my head dry and shiny, freshly washed. I couldn't bear the immensity of the sky and looked down. The city, sullen and empty, lay deflated under my echoing footsteps. On a night like that, it stops sprawling upwards; instead, it topples over on its back like a hibernating beast, horizontal, forcing its infinity on my ant-like crawl. I inspected the cracks in the pavement, vaguely hoping to find a key to their intricate pattern, which I sensed would be less inscrutable than the enigmatic blueprint of the starry void above me. But the meaning of both eluded me.

I remembered the pain of a year ago. That's when I lost my last job and I've been looking for a new one ever since, but nothing has panned out. People in the old job humiliated me. And I wouldn't have it. I might starve but I won't tolerate the slightest sign of disrespect. Ever since then I've got into the habit of roaming the streets. I think I was vaguely looking for a miracle in the low-lying winter-frozen spaces of the city: a chance encounter, perhaps, a freak opportunity that would never stroll into the four walls of my drab attic that I'd come to loathe.

What I met through my nocturnal wanderings was the wind. Indiscriminately, using the props afforded to it by every season, it piled up spectral slabs of chaos on the sidewalk. In autumn it sated on leaves – dispersing, then spinning them into ephemeral castles. In summer it clogged the passageways between houses with mobile hordes of dust and crumpled balls of paper; it leafed through the fat weekend *Le Devoir* editions page after page, exposing stale news to the indifferent legs of passersby.

In winter, when there was no snow, and the unswept leaves, dark and oblong, like ancient Egyptian boats, got frozen solid into the ground, the wind's credibility hung solely on aimless phantoms like myself. It fingered my spine under my shabby loose coat, vertebra after vertebra, all the way down to the tail bone, till it found an exit through the hole in my pocket.

Just like the wind, I kept up an appearance of movement under the monotonous absence of change. In order to stretch my dwindling budget, I moved from one crummy room to another, all the time staying put, so to speak. All these rooms were carbon copies of each other: all on the top floor, right under the roof. They all had wallpaper of an indefinable color coming off at the junction with the ceiling and most had showers that didn't work. Since I was often late with my rent, I kept my mouth shut about the shower and didn't wash for days.

I wish the wind would stop. Its aimless wanderings disturb me. Sometimes I fantasize about my city. I imagine that in the past it was all soft and pliable: wax-like gyrating staircases climbing along the faces of the houses; the houses themselves soft, framed with trees, lithe like lianas. Then, I imagined, the wind came along and stiffened all form, so that nothing was left from the initial design. Skeletal branches knock against the window panes along the dark façades.

I even imagined that the cracks in the crooked sidewalks were also the wind's work; that the wind had slanted the pavement towards the middle of the road and swept the few pedestrians away; now people walk in the middle of the road, forcing the infrequent cars to swerve into the oncoming lane to pass them.

I too gingerly step into the middle of the road. I give nothing of myself to the city. And the city closes on me, begrudging me every speck of itself, till one day I finally venture to a real Saturday *milonga*. And that changes my life.

3

At first, to avoid embarrassment, I decided to ask only the beginners to dance, leaving some possibility of an escape in case I completely screwed it up. But I was mistaken in my strategy; though good dancers were seeking out partners of equal skills, there were many other forces at play that I couldn't quite grasp at the time, and which I still don't understand. There would be a girl – a young, smooth, insipid creature – hardly able to make two coherent steps, in the arms of an experienced, even excellent dancer, usually an older man. Perhaps, I, too, in the inversion of roles, could ask a good dancer without feeling I was going to crack.

At my first party I felt elated. I liked the muted ambiance: the flicker of candles on each table; the smell of perfume on the women's heated skin mixed with cigarette smoke reaching the floor from the stairwell where people smoked between *tandos,* two or three dances forming one theme. The fact that I could always go to the bar, have a glass of beer or whisky and watch others dance in case I suddenly got cold feet, suited me just fine. I liked the way men quickly sprayed breath freshener into their mouths before inviting a woman onto the dance floor and then put the spray away into their breast pocket with the same quick, clandestine gesture. I liked the provocativeness of the women's outfits; their black shimmering skirts with slits at the side that bared their fishnet-stockinged thighs; their see-through tops held in place on the flimsiest promise of an imperceptible strap. I liked the way women closed their eyes while dancing, as if in complete abandon. Sensations overwhelmed me; the most powerful of all was the heat, coming from my partners' bodies after I danced two or three tangos in a row. Some women felt like balls of fire, all burning and melting inside, my only protection a layer of clothes – the silk, the velvet, the chiffon. Underneath the fabric I could feel the clasp of their bras.

I instinctively avoided placing my hand on women's naked backs (I noticed that other men did the same), and moved it to the area safely protected by fabric. But once, inadvertently, my hand slipped up my partner's bare shoulder-blades: they were cold and sticky with sweat. I was struck by the unpleasantness of the sensation.

If my right hand, always resting on my partner's back, had some level of defence (no mater how light and transparent the fabric usually felt), then the left was completely exposed, and I semi-consciously hoped for the exchange of some silent messages, some mysterious current traveling from her fingers to mine … But nothing was communicated to me and I was disappointed.

Dancing the tango I discovered how different women's hands felt: some very soft, others dry and rough as men's. What kind of lives might women with such hands have had?

Then there was the sensation of their breasts. In *calesita* women leaned over me at a sharp angle, their bodies linked to mine at the chest. It was a never-ebbing excitement to feel the weight of a woman's body so publicly placed on top of mine. Some women's breasts felt small and firm, some were big and soft, and I learnt to transport the tactile sensors from my fingers to my torso; not an unpleasant experience, misplaced as it might seem.

Two women in particular attracted my attention.

One, in claret-colored tight pants and a tunic, with a pale face and emaciated, almost breastless body, had a languid, careless way of moving. She danced obliviously, as if divorced from her own self. Her long ash-blond braid, too, seemed to have a life of its own, only remotely echoing the turns and twists of its owner. I was mesmerized by these double unsynchronized rondos, the way this ankle-reaching snake lightly swept against the floor when the woman suddenly went into a deep lunge. When I finally plucked up my courage to approach her, fish-like unsmiling eyes transfixed me. I thought what an excellent dancer she was, in her strange, inflexible, rake-like way. Yes, in my mind, I thought of her as a rake, and was both repulsed and attracted by her. She was staring right through me. What would it feel like to hold her in my arms? The more I desired her, the less I was capable of inviting her.

And then there was another girl, almost as tall as me, with wide hips and chocolate skin that brought the azure waves of the Caribbean to lap at my feet; I started walking towards her, but she was quickly intercepted by another man; and then I watched the oily smoothness of her dance, and I imagined her in my, not another man's arms. Sometimes she was a goddess, and sometimes a mysterious creature out of the depths of the ocean, a mollusc in search of its form, and I was the shell that could absorb her and give her this form, had she only trusted me with her exquisitely slow undulations.

The music stopped. At that moment the yellow band holding the Carib girl's voluminous hair back slipped off her head, and she bent over to pick it up with a careless gesture. She was now an ordinary girl perhaps, accessible. Desire burned inside me.

"Would you like to dance?" a high, somewhat childish voice broke into my reverie.

"Sure," I replied to the owner of this voice, who, to my surprise, turned out to be a short, middle-aged woman. I hadn't noticed her approach.

Must be in her late forties, early fifties, I thought. Much shorter than me (a disadvantage in dancing), but it was the first time that a woman had invited me for a dance, and I felt flattered.

"My name is Catherine," she said.

"I'm Jason."

I was trying to catch the beat of the music before making the first step.

"Have you been dancing for a long time?"

"Oh no, I'm a beginner."

"That's all right. It takes a while, but you'll learn, you'll see."

I was slightly annoyed, first, at her patronizing kindness, but more by the fact that she needed to talk to me at all while we danced: it prevented me from concentrating on my steps. Her bleached blond ringlets were at the level of my chin. I didn't see much of her face or her body, but she felt cosy and feminine in my arms, with those neat unhurried steps of hers. As if she were crocheting something with her small feet. I noticed her wasp-like waist neatly emphasized by a tight black belt that set off her generous hips. I also liked the feel of her fuchsia dress; it was soft, old-fashioned, with loose translucent sleeves falling all the way to her shoulders when she raised her well-shaped arms. A row of small pearly buttons rose to an upright collar that left only a small wedge of flesh at the top of her neck exposed. There was something touching about her being so old-fashioned. As I was leading her into forward *ochos*, I caught a glimpse of her knee: it was smooth and round, a gently outlined slope that seemed to be completely boneless. Catherine's whole body didn't have one sharp line; her shoulders and her chest were cosily plump, and fitted perfectly in my arms, in spite of the fact that she was so much shorter than me.

While dancing with her, I became aware of a peculiar

fragrance. It wasn't the smell of perfume – I don't think she was wearing any – but rather, the smell of her skin. It reminded me of something remote, long forgotten, and I couldn't figure out what it was. Then, in a flash, in cadence with the music, an old country house in England came back to me.

In the year of my mother's death, my aunt took me there to spend a summer with her. I was ten years old and we were slicing up juicy green apples from our garden and spreading them over towels on the floor of our little shack at the back of the property. I thought then that they looked like small round moons, those apples, but later, when the air cooled down, and the real moon and the stars came out, we had a sudden visitor: a hedgehog came trotting along with the heavy tread of a trooper. He rolled onto the apples, hooking onto his needles as many he could. Then he disappeared. Catherine's skin smelled like those slightly withered apples, twenty years ago, in the August of my mother's death.

While dancing, Catherine didn't fuss around on the floor, nor did she press me into constant movement. I could stop and relax to the point of not thinking about my steps anymore. Most of that evening we danced together, and I felt no need to change partners.

But when I got home after midnight, I felt completely spent. Taking off my shirt, I saw a damp spot on my upper sleeve left by Catherine's armpit. The smell of apples haunted me.

I was soon spending my days in anticipation of the weekends. My head was filled with scraps of music and vague yearnings for Catherine whom I now danced with regularly. One night was particularly disturbing; I dreamt about making love to her incessantly. When I saw her the next Saturday at the dance studio, I felt embarrassed and invited other women to dance instead. When I finally danced with her, I avoided looking into her eyes.

Between dances Catherine and I hardly talked to each other. I knew nothing about her life, my arms knew her body, but otherwise we remained complete strangers. I liked this anonymous intimacy of the tango. I found the physical proximity to a woman who was old enough to be my mother exhilarating. It intrigued me, and raised me up in my own eyes. I felt like an iceberg, the whole of which nobody, not even me, could see.

Catherine was one of those rare, superlative dancers who wasn't flashy on the floor, but could intuit your slightest move.

At a special *milonga* the night before Christmas Eve, we danced far beyond midnight till the candles were extinguished and the chairs put up on the tables. We came out into the street and were confronted by a ferocious gust of wind.

"Where do you live?" Catherine asked.

"Ten blocks away from here, on Park Avenue," I lied. I didn't want her to know that I had no car and had walked across half the city to get to the *milonga*: it was late and the buses had stopped running.

"I'm driving in that direction. I can give you a ride."

"Well, I could walk ... but sure, if it's not out of your way." Climbing into her white car, I noticed a pair of crutches on the front seat next to her. She must have read a silent question in my eyes.

"I fell down and broke my ankle. That was a couple of months ago and now it's much better."

I recalled then, through the unconscious memory of my arm, that in *ocho* Catherine would lose her balance for a split second and lean more heavily than needed on my arm. She did have that imperceptible limp.

"It must hurt you when you dance?" I asked.

"It hurts some, but I'm used to it now. Another three weeks, the doctor said, and it'll be completely healed."

What a devotion to the tango, I thought, and what endurance! A hard little nut in spite of her delicate looks.

"Could you stop right at that corner, near this building, please? I live over there," I pointed to a nondescript façade that I thought could pose for my apartment.

"It was wonderful dancing with you tonight," she said hugging me good-bye. She pressed her body to mine, and I held her for a minute, postponing the inevitability of having to get out of the car. I wanted to continue what we had started on the dance floor, though I wasn't sure what that might be. Perhaps, making love. So, I kept holding her.

"I know it's late, but I wish I could dance one last time with you ... Today is Christmas Eve. We should celebrate ..." I whispered in her ear, taking in the sweat mixed with apple fragrance again.

"What if we go to ... I mean, would you mind if ... I have some good CDs, but my sound system is not working ... I mean, it's in the shop ... In the meantime, could we not, perhaps, dance at your place?" I ventured.

She gently freed herself from my arms and paused. Then she turned off the engine. We were now sitting in the car in darkness. There was no sound, except the wind gnarling at the car's flanks.

"I suppose we could," Catherine said finally without looking at me. "But it's late now and I'm tired." She paused again. "I need to go to work in the morning."

"Catherine," I almost lost my voice, "you're the most beautiful woman I've ever met. Dancing with you is like ... it's really very powerful! I can't imagine waiting till next Saturday."

"Oh, please ..." She chuckled, then patted me on the cheek: "You don't need to flatter me, you know. I'm an old woman ..."

"What has age to do with all that?" I said vehemently. "You have experience. You have that special beauty of maturity ... And you're a wonderful dancer!"

"Oh that – perhaps!"

"Don't ever say you're old, even as a joke." I caressed her hand. Catherine laughed faintly but didn't remove her hand.

"I'm not that old, just old enough to be your mother."

I took away my hand, moving away from her. She gave me a long sideways look.

"Well, let me see. We could stop over for a cup of tea at my place. For a very brief while," she said with averted eyes.

"Yes, for a brief while," I replied. I reached for her chin, turned her face towards me and kissed her. Her lips felt soft. She didn't resist. While she was driving, I put my hand on her knee.

We were now in Westmount, and she finally parked the car in the driveway of an old Edwardian house. While she fumbled for the keys in her purse, I stared at the stained glass in the porch door. Not shitty. She has a good life, this woman. I wiped my feet on the doormat, a straw elephant dangling a WELCOME sign in his trunk.

Inside, I smelled a suffocating mixture of dried flowers, baked pies and the familiar fermenting apples. It was warm, even stifling, as if the house was seldom aired. The hallway was full of antique low tables, chiffoniers, baskets. A bouquet of tulips splayed out of an elephant-shaped vase served as a lamp. Each tulip was made of colored glass, with a bulb inside. I noticed that there were no Christmas decorations of any sort.

"Would you like some tea? I don't drink wine so late at night. Wake up with a headache tomorrow," she said.

"Tea is fine," I said.

I followed her to the kitchen. There I found myself in an elephant kingdom run amuck. Gaudy beasts with trunks lifted like trumpets winked from the tea towels, curtains and tablecloths. There was a tiny elephant sitting on top of each canister; there were elephant mugs and pots and cups on the shelves. The tea cosy was an elephant and so were the backs of the chairs around the table. Two of the four chairs were occupied by huge stuffed beasts with erect trunks, all four pillar-like legs up in the air. One beast was pink, the other blue. The blue one was staring at me, the pink one at Catherine.

"It'll take a couple of minutes before the kettle boils. What kind of tea would you like?" she asked, leaning against a cushion where two crocheted beasts intertwined their trunks like the copulating snakes on the caduceus.

Under the bright kitchen light Catherine looked much older than in the semi-darkness of the dance studio. She was obviously tired. Her smudged make-up revealed all the trappings of age: the swelling under the eyes, the deep wrinkles around her nose, the sagging skin of her cheek-bones. Perhaps aware of the effect that her face had on me, she turned off the overhead light, and lit two candles.

Two sharp shadows reached the middle of her cheeks with their narrow tongues, then licked her nose, her lips, cutting her face into swiftly moving triangles.

"Your elephant collection is quite remarkable. I've never seen anything like it," I said, avoiding looking at her.

"These are not mine. They're my ex-husband's. We traveled a lot. We lived in India for several years and there he took up carving. Elephants were easy to make and we brought back quite a few. Friends assumed we collected them. For each birthday party or anniversary somebody would bring us an elephant. And then I guess we fell into this trap and started looking out for them in different countries. Some are made of real ebony, some copper, there are even a couple gold ones ... More than six hundred in this house," she said. "Would you like one?"

She got up and reached to a small shelf where a family of black elephants was walking trunk to tail along a crocheted meadow towards the frosted window. She removed the smallest baby elephant, last in the file, and handed it over to me. I slipped it into my pocket.

Catherine poured tea out into two elephant cups.

"Have you ever had your palm read?" Catherine asked, sipping at her cup. "This is one thing I'm really good at. If I look at your hand, I can tell everything about your character, your past and your future. Give me your hand." She held my hand in both of hers; her clasp was cosy and warm.

"Oh, what a big palm! Nice shape, too! You've had

a hard life," she said, gently unfolding my index finger. It's because you're a dreamer and an artist. You're very impressionable, very soft inside."

"How do you know?" I smiled and drew her closer to me. She stroked my hair.

"The palm tells it all. See, between the valleys of Venus and Mars there is a little mound, and then there is a line, separating those two valleys. Yours is very deep. Only artists have it."

"Can you foretell the future as well?"

"Yes, there is lots of traveling ahead ..."

"Traveling and big fortune, right?" I laughed. "They always say that. Do you really believe in this?"

"Big fortune, hmm ... that I don't know. But traveling, that's for sure. Look!" She showed me some more lines on my palm.

"Where should I go? Is that also written on my palm? How about going to Buenos Aires together?" I now took her hand into mine and pretended I was studying it.

"Let's see if your hand says you agree to travel with me. This line, right?"

"It's not that simple," she laughed. "You have to look for a pattern, not just one line ..."

"All I want to see is if you're going on a trip to Buenos Aires with me," I said half-jokingly. "That's all I care about."

"Oh, don't be silly!" She puffed up her cheeks and,

with a little smack of her lips, let the air out coquettishly. She was suddenly acting like a little girl.

"No really, I'm dead serious! If I have to travel, why don't you come with me? Everybody goes to Buenos Aires: Alfredo, Jorge. The whole gang. Sebastian has a place people can stay. I think he's turned his own house into a hostel for tango people. And he doesn't charge that much."

She looked at me with a mixture of surprise and incredulity.

"Are you serious? You're talking about it, Jason, as if it was, I don't know, a ride to the Laurentians or to Toronto, at most. Just hop on a plane, and you're there. Plus," she hesitated a moment, "we hardly know each other."

"So, that'll give us a chance to get to know each other better ..."

"You are a dreamer, I was right about that!" She was laughing now in an easy, light-hearted way. I had obviously managed to amuse her. But she didn't take me seriously, I could see that, yet I persisted.

"Look, it's not impossible. We just have to plan ahead. You said you work? I mean, can you take a leave?"

"Sure, I work. My next vacation isn't till September."

"So, we'll go in September. It's nice there in September, not too hot; the tourist season will be over. It would be wonderful, I promise!" Her girlish laugh excited me.

"Well, then?"

I saw that part of her wanted to be persuaded. I moved closer to her and took her in my arms. I couldn't restrain myself and started kissing her neck, her hands. My breath was short.

"We'll walk down those streets in Buenos Aires, the same barrios where our tango started ..."

I said "our" as if we already had some mutual history, as if our life was just a continuation of what started generations ago in the Southside docks and brothels of Buenos Aires and all I had to do now was to resuscitate this life together with her.

"Don't think about money. I'll get what we need from my cousin in Toronto, he has a shoe store and he is rich." I was lying, I had no cousin with or without money, but I wanted her badly. "Please, Catherine, say yes!"

I put my hand on her smooth knee showing through the slit of her skirt. I had wanted to touch this knee for a long time. Words poured out of me, uncontrollably, rapidly.

"I want to hold you in my arms forever, I want to carry you – to protect you ... I don't care what people would say ... I've always been looking for a woman like you."

"Oh, stop it. It is just tango, that's all there is!"

"Why don't you believe me?" I desperately wanted to make love to her.

"I believe you, all right, I believe you!" She suddenly started to sob.

"What's the matter? Why are you crying?"

"I'm sorry, this is silly. I'm really sorry."

"Did I hurt you?"

"No, Jason. It has nothing to do with you. It's been a year today since my husband left me. Anniversaries are hard."

"How could he have left such a wonderful woman? Especially at Christmas?"

What I said was stupid, of course, and I meant it as a joke, but my hands were working up her black-stockinged leg, words were popping out of me, and I didn't care about them anymore.

Catherine quickly removed my hand from her knee and pulled the two parts of her skirt together. When she burst into tears I was completely confused. I never know how to deal with female tears. To me they're a punch below the belt; a plea for help that hardly leaves me any room to manoeuvre, urging me to act without telling me what I'm supposed to do. They make me feel guilty. But what am I to blame for? That her husband left her? That the world is such a fucked-up place? I didn't create it, it's not my responsibility.

"Were you married a long time?' I couldn't think of anything else to say.

"Almost twenty years. They were happy years, we never quarrelled, not once." There was a pressing, raw sincerity in her voice.

"It must have been hard on you. But all that's in the past. Forget about it. It's time to turn over a new leaf. We'll be together now." I surprised myself at my own words. I needed to convince myself by sealing my promises with action, so I scooped her into my arms and started to undo the upper buttons of her blouse. She resisted.

"Don't," she said dryly. "Don't."

"Why not? Please ..." My voice became coarse, a stranger's voice.

"Don't, I'm telling you."

But it was too late. While my left hand was traveling down her back in the attempt to undo her bra, my right hand dipped under the bra's wire. Oh, the delicious sensation of soft female flesh! One more second ... and I pulled my hand away in disgust. Instead of the breast, I had run into a flat surface, hard as a board.

"What's that?" I asked, not trusting my own hand anymore.

"It's what's left after the surgery," she said calmly

Stupefied, I imagined red and blue tissues, all in knots. A mixture of horror and cold curiosity suddenly took hold of me.

"Show me."

"No."

"Let me touch it, then."

"No. Please don't. This is why my husband left me."

"Because of that?

"Yes. Two weeks after the surgery."

I unclenched her fingers grasping her blouse. Yes, I had to see it for myself.

Removing her top I gently ran my finger over her former breast, first the left one, then the right. Strangely, it wasn't as horrible as I expected. There merely were no breasts anymore, just a flat surface, much like the chest of a man. There was even a residual layer of fat left, between bone and skin. How cleverly she had camouflaged it while dancing with me, I thought.

I felt a sudden overwhelming sense of fatigue, as if something had changed in the air. Perhaps the wind had abated. It was eerily quiet. Catherine slipped the top back on, leaving the padded bra where it had fallen on the floor.

"It's late. It's time for me to go," I said.

"Yes, of course. Shall I give you a ride?" asked Catherine.

"No, thanks. I need to walk a little. It'll be good for me to walk."

"I understand … I know you live far away … though you said you live nearby. Sure you don't need a ride?"

How did she know? But I felt too tired to think. After all, I'd danced well past midnight. It'd been a very long day, and frankly I didn't care.

"Merry Christmas to you," I said.

"Merry Christmas," she responded. Then she closed the door behind me.

I took in my first gulp of fresh air. Then wiped my feet against the straw elephant holding out to me his "WELCOME" trunk. That was weird. I wasn't coming. I was going. But then everything felt weird at that hour of the wolf on Christmas Eve. Tango seemed repulsive to me now. And I couldn't fathom what on earth had moved me to squander my last money on it. Tango was a deceit, a chimera. Women were a chimera. So was life.

I walked out into the street gasping for the crisp, frosty air that felt like a special gift for my oxygen-starved lungs. The delicious fragrant chill caressed my skin. Oh, the joy of escape, of moving again wherever one pleased in brisk carefree steps!

It didn't bother me in the slightest that I had to cross half the city to get to my place. I became aware that something had indeed changed around me. A strange quietness clad the city, as if something was cut short in mid-phrase. Yes, the wind had stopped. The wind that had been whistling down the streets for months, that wind had dropped its daggers and left the city. Gone, as suddenly as it had arrived, replaced by white spectral mourners that had alighted on the ground in complete silence, whirling around broodingly, powdering the city with snow; frosting trees, shrubs, porches and the sharp peaks of the fences; cushioning sidewalks, and sweeping over the minute untidy indecencies that the wind had randomly left.

Within half an hour, the city was fully dressed in its new attire; it lay there in solemn purity, white and sinless. It seemed to become lighter with each thrust of snow, as if ready to ascend. I, too, felt that I could rise to the skies, all I had to do was to get rid of the ballast that kept me earthbound.

Slipping my freezing hands into my pockets, I felt something smooth and solid. Catherine's baby elephant still retained the warmth of the house I'd just left, much warmer than my hand. I held it for a minute before throwing it into a freshly blown mound of snow. Softly it sank down into the white shroud, legs and trunk up, making no more then a dent. I stood and watched it quickly disappear under the abundant whiteness falling from the night sky.

It was almost four in the morning when I finally reached home.

4

In spite of the fact that I wanted to let go of tango, tango didn't let go of me. On the contrary, its grip tightened as time passed. It took me another three years to become an excellent tango dancer. I met people and made connections in the tango community that finally helped me land a well-paying job. As a travelling sales agent, selling everything from shoelaces to toy dinosaurs, I travelled a lot on business through Europe and South America, using every opportunity to dance tango wherever I could. When I finally arrived in Buenos Aires it proved different from what I'd expected. Perhaps the time wasn't right: a deep recession had struck the country. I found little Latin American warmth there. The people were aloof, even arrogant. Perhaps reality can never live up to the Buenos Aires in my dreams, which should be left there, intact.

I danced tango in Paris and London, in Munich, and Prague. Tango, I discovered, was popular in the most unexpected places: who would think, for example, that cold Finns would take to it so passionately? Their style was very different, though, from anybody else's. They were a kind of brooding, melancholic bunch. And they danced in a sort of poetic way. But it was sad poetry.

It was there, in Helsinki, in one of their *milongas*, that I met up with a woman strikingly resembling Catherine, a younger version of her. I felt an immediate twinge in my heart, a wave of the old desire. But then I remembered the Christmas night in the elephant house and felt a residue of old disgust, even anger. I wanted to hide, but the woman smiled at me, which I interpreted as an invitation for a dance. I was a new face in this milieu and I guess she wanted to check me out.

We got talking and it turned out the woman was

Catherine's daughter. Who says life isn't full of surprises! She was married to a Finnish engineer and lived in the backcountry, four hundred miles from Helsinki. She and her husband were tango aficionados, and once a month traveled half a day to make it to the capital for a dance. The daughter had the same gentle touch, the same sense of cosiness in tango as her mother. Her footwork, as I recall now, was even more intricate.

"You look very much like your mother," I said.

"Oh," she responded, surprised. "You knew my mother?"

"Yes, a while ago in Montreal. We used to go to the same studio. I don't know if she remembers me, but in any case, say hello to her from me, next time you see her."

The daughter gave me a strange look and suddenly stumbled. I was surprised. I thought she was a better dancer. I was giving her quite a strong lead.

"My mother died several years ago," she said.

My feet suddenly froze as if I was an apprentice again. I lowered my eyes.

"Oh, I'm sorry to hear that," I pressed out of myself, finally. "I knew she had been ill … But I didn't know she had passed away."

The daughter lifted her face and looked me straight in the eyes. Her hand slipped down my shoulder.

"So you knew my mother well, then?"

"Oh, not really, we just danced a couple of times,

that's all. But people in the community kind of knew ... well, somebody must have told me about her condition. Actually, it was my girlfriend, she had it too, and then she took up tango and kayaking, yes, kayaking and tango, we both actually took up tango. That really helped her ..."

"And how is your girlfriend now?" asked Catherine's daughter.

"Who? Oh, she's fine, thank you. Eh-h. Cured. I mean, tango has completely cured her."

"Well, my mother had an excellent prognosis after the surgery. No metastases. She could have lived, had it not been for this terrible accident."

We were standing now in the middle of the floor, two cliffs in a smoothly flowing stream of couples spinning around us.

"Oh, really?" I said, continuing to stare at my partner.

"Happened just before Christmas ... It'll be three years this Christmas. She called in to work to say she wasn't feeling well. But three hours later, they found her on the street hit by a car.

"At Christmas there's lots of drunk driving going on. Like, everybody gets drunk," I said.

"No, the driver was totally sober, but, apparently, he didn't see my mother in the blizzard. There was a strong wind. We think she might have slipped."

"That's terrible." I said, "I'm really sorry to hear that. Your mother was a wonderful dancer, and I'm sure a wonderful person, too." But I didn't know what else to say, and tried to change the subject.

"How is tango in Helsinki?"

"It's just fine, my husband and I love it," Catherine's daughter replied. "But we don't get a chance to dance too often. We have a small child, and in winter it's hard to get out of the backwoods. The days are so short."

"Come to Canada sometime. You must know Montreal's become world class for tango. Big tango scene. You can dance every night. I simply couldn't imagine living in a city without tango now."

"Yes, I suppose it would be difficult," the daughter said. "For a dancer as good as you, I imagine it would be. We were thinking of moving to Montreal some time in the future when our daughter grows up a bit."

"That would be terrific!" I said, leading her into *sacada*, moving into her space and displacing her leg with mine. But she didn't respond. In the middle of the dance she stood frozen.

"I've inherited my mother's house. Full of elephants." Her lips folded in a sad semi-chuckle. Her eyes slid into space, somewhere beyond my shoulder.

"When you come to Montreal, give me a buzz. I'll show you around the city ... I mean, you know the city of course, but maybe I can introduce you to people at a *milonga*." I felt in my jacket pocket for my Parker fountain pen, tore a page out of my datebook and jotted down my phone number.

"That's kind of you," said Catherine's daughter, taking the piece of paper. Her nails were smooth, with pink polish.

I noticed that one of my shoelaces was undone, so I didn't wait for the music to stop, and accompanied Catherine's daughter to her seat. I bent over to tie the laces, then went across the room to ask another girl to dance. That girl was wearing a short blue dress. I really love that color. It looked so cute on her.

Carmelita

1

I came here two years ago, shortly after my father's death. More than anytime before, I felt then at loose ends in spite of the large inheritance I so suddenly came into. Turning into a rich man in the blink of an eye may present certain difficulties for someone who has been a 'disheveled loser' all his life, as my father habitually called me from the age of five, referring, no doubt, both to my frazzled hair, not a strand of which I possess now, and my inability to put to any good use the strange talents that I somehow managed to tease out of my indifferent and negligent fate. I think it was this little bouquet of quirks lurking in the fissures of my brain and disguising themselves as the early signs of *wunderkinderism* that prevented me later in life from mastering any worthwhile profession. The ability to multiply five-digit numbers in my head is one example of my arcane and totally futile gifts. It used to be a sure bait for the girls I fancied, if only for a few dashing moments of initial acquaintance, when – pencil in hand – they'd quickly sketch a neat scaffold on a scrap of paper, verify the results and then turn their sharp-chinned, sun-lit faces towards me in complete disbelief. "I can also do roots. Give me any number." Puzzled, they'd walk around me, a curiosity under a museum glass, pause for a moment and then flit off like sated birds from a feeder to join their rope-skipping flock in the schoolyard.

My other gift was my photographic memory, keeping intact page after page of books I had read twenty years earlier. As a teenager I stammered, but my most ingenious classmates laid siege to this predicament, teasing the string of battle dates and names of the generals out of me at the exams they forced me to write for them. For a while, my lopsided usefulness did keep at bay their desire to punch me the moment my round form got into their field of vision.

It was only by fluke that at the age of thirty I finally stumbled on something that could bring me a semblance of an income: it turned out I could make up elaborate stories and fables at the drop of a hat. (At one point I secretly fancied myself a writer, even a poet, though I couldn't show a single written page for my whimsy.) But people in the street didn't care about my misapprehensions when I'd appear on a busy corner, cap for coins on the sidewalk, and, strumming three strings on a banjo, follow the meandering paths of my imagination. "One word, ladies and gentlemen, give me one word," I nudged the onlookers, for it was all I needed to start spreading the magic carpet of my fantasies under the busy and indifferent feet of the city. I preferred concrete words over abstract ones, and women over men, for women were a much more generous and empathetic audience for a lost soul like me. I liked women's bodies, and the way they moved; I liked their twitter, their quick shift of subjects, their wide-eyed compassion towards the hurting ones, and the girlish playfulness that illuminated with sudden innocence even the oldest and the most lived-in faces of their tribe.

Unfortunately, women didn't pay me back in the same coin. Was it my natural shyness or my appearance that deterred them? Yes, I am a short and rather heavy-built man with bulging eyes positioned wide apart on a head too massive for my smallish body. In spite of that, women always told me I had some charm, if only because they sensed I was ready to serve them. And – oh, my pathetic self-pity! – how many men with far less pleasing exteriors had I watched becoming happy husbands and fathers! I, on the other hand, was destined to live and die alone.

It was this final realization that elevated my fears of death to a degree of paranoia. I've heard that people who haven't used up the full measure of their lives have a hard time dying. Remorse must make the physical pain of passing into the Neverland unbearable. That's when it dawned upon me that I, for one, hadn't even started living, for I couldn't, in full honesty, count as life the tediousness and the boredom of days that had filled up sixty years of my existence. In a nutshell, I suddenly became afraid of the pain of dying! There must be some way out of this fear, I was saying to myself during the long sleepless nights I was by now quite accustomed to. And I began to hope, in a very childish manner, that the love of one woman, never experienced by me yet, could deliver me from the fears of the final passing ... Oh, the dreams of an old decrepit man! Get back to reality, my father had been hammering into my head all his life, and then, finally, his call reached my ears in the form of a huge inheritance that I reluctantly, against all my instincts, had to deal with.

This shift in my life was as unexpected as it was immediate: suddenly, a man in whose existence nobody had shown the slightest interest, became the longed-for target of an invisible, smiling, finger-crooking crowd. I began to receive invitations for dinners, gala concerts and charity events. (I never owned a suit, nor a tie, so I had to get both to show up at the functions organized by my father's retinue.) The phone barking at me out of the corner of my half-empty apartment became my worst enemy. Needless to say, I would never think of getting a cell. The sight of sealed envelopes oppressed me. Like Satie, the composer, I stopped opening my mail.

It was at that point that I decided to drop everything, and guided by mere chance rather than choice, came here to Zipolite, a small Mexican village tucked away on the Pacific Coast. I was looking for some meaningful way of getting rid of my money, if that oxymoron makes any sense – well, it did then to me: an orphanage, a hospital for sick children, or a school for the handicapped lurked in my imagination as a summary rescuing plan of sorts.

Zipolite consisted of only one street lined with dilapidated bungalows and stalls roofed with palm leaves where Indians from the hills laid out their trinkets. This humble, yet nonchalant life strangely suited my mood. As the daytime heat receded, the local beauties came strolling along the main drag mixing with stray dogs and barefoot toddlers; a fat American with a shiny skull, owner of two local hotels, watched the crowd out of his hammock on the balcony of his *El Paraiso*. At night, in the back yards, villagers burned their *basura*. Plastic bags, containers and leftovers morphed into black pillars of stench that crawled over the beach, reaching further and further out into the ocean. Old tires provided an atavistic entertainment for the local youth who burned them every night in bonfires dotting the beach line. Till dawn, the air was unbreathable, and I was coughing away through the nights, struggling with insomnia. Days were no better: sinking into a sweaty drowsiness, I was asking myself why on earth I had come to this forsaken village.

One late afternoon, unusual noises outside jerked me out of my slumber. I went downstairs, past the hammocks bulging with sun-tanning vacationers, past the vendors, to the ocean front. Part of the beach was sealed off with a red ribbon the agitated crowd was pushing impatiently against. I couldn't understand what excited these people: my eyes could see nothing but the expanse of the ocean beyond that ribbon. A man in a white shirt shouted in Spanish into a loudspeaker. I noticed that everybody in the crowd was holding something in their outstretched hands. I came up closer.

And then I saw her. She was on her haunches, on the other side of the ribbon separating the crowd from the smooth hard sand of the surf. While the agitated forward-pressing mass was facing the empty ocean, she alone was facing the crowd; there was movement all around her; she alone was still, except for her hair – a magnificent jet-black waterfall cascading all the way down to her thighs. With a strong thrust of breeze her hair suddenly transformed itself into a wild bird, then took off from her shoulders, spread its wings, soared, and then landed again on her back; for the first time then I saw her face. It revealed an austere and proud beauty: the chiseled cheekbones, the perfect arch of her eyebrows, the aquiline nose gave her both an air of arrogance and a fragile aloofness. There was grace in her stillness, but also loneliness.

The daughter of an ancient Indian priest must have looked like that, I thought. But there must be mixed blood, the blood of Spaniards, Moors and Jews running in the veins of her ancestors as well. She was young, not more than thirty.

Unaware of being watched, the girl herself was watching the crowd through a camera she had improvised out of her index finger and a thumb.

"*Buenas Tardes,*" I greeted her, squatting inadvertently inside her fingers-framed world. She scrutinized me silently through her camera. I smiled and mimicked her gesture with my fingers. She put her hand down.

"I don't really speak Spanish. *Buenas tardes* and *adiós* are about the only words I know. Do you speak English, by any chance?"

"I certainly do, but you're in my way," she answered with a splendid confidence and got up to her feet. As she was rising, I noticed a small diamond pendulum nestling between her half-bare breasts. On fire from the setting sun, it caught my eye with sharp multicolored sparks. Her wrap-around skirt tightly hugged her narrow hips, concealing her legs but leaving her flat belly exposed.

With her elongated El Greco limbs and neck she stood considerably taller than me.

"You speak with a British accent. Where did you learn your English?"

She brushed her long hair aside and paused, examining me.

"Studied at the London Institute of Art for five years," she finally said.

"You're an artist then?"

She kept looking at me without saying a word.

I realized it was the expression of her strangely still, almond-shaped eyes that more than anything else gave her that air of aloofness. She looked at me through a thicket of dark lashes without squinting. If the ocean was capable of gazing at humans from its mysterious depths, it would be gazing out of these eyes. What softened the air of severity about her, though, was her skin and her mouth: the skin had an olive tinge, magically warm in the setting sun. Her mouth was moving, as if she was savoring the sight not with her eyes but with her sensual, bow-like lips.

Nodding to the crowd, I asked my new acquaintance what was going on. "They are releasing baby turtles into the ocean. They do it every year, at the sunset."

"Where do they get so many?"

"Hatch them in the village," she said indifferently.

"*La causa noble de la liberación de las tortugas permite a los miembros orgullosos de la comunidad …* " barked a megaphone.

"What is he saying?"

"The noble cause of liberating the turtles will allow all the members of the community … I didn't get it … to proudly go to hell, I suppose."

For the first time I heard her laugh.

"Is it your first time in Mexico?" she asked then.

"It is."

Momentarily I felt embarrassed at being a stranger in her country.

"Mexicans are like children. They like entertainment and will pay to be told how great they are. Out of two hundred turtles one may survive."

"Do you know why they release these creatures at sunset?" I asked.

"No clue, nor do I care."

"Yet, you, too, came to watch the event."

"I came to watch people … I don't care much about turtles."

"You must be a photographer then, though I never saw anybody taking pictures with such a camera … " I smiled. But she didn't take me up on it.

"I'm not a photographer. I'm a painter," she said seriously.

"Well, isn't it close?"

"Opposite mediums."

She was abrupt and I didn't know how to keep up the conversation.

As soon as the sun sank into the ocean, the man in the white shirt cut the ribbon and people rushed towards the water, their tiny charges in their palms. They placed the baby turtles on the wet sand bared by a receding wave. The turtles froze stiff, shocked by their first contact with the elements. Finally, a wave washed some of them off into the ocean, but others, still paralyzed, had to be carried into the water. My eyes followed their first helpless movements: it seemed inconceivable that these tiny clots of life would survive their first night in the cold abyss.

The girl turned around and started walking away along the water's edge. The incoming wave licked the hem of her dress and she raised her skirt over her knees. Her legs were perfectly shaped. I found myself following her.

"By the way, my name is Joseph Parson. I'm from Canada. And your name is?" I caught up with her and tried to keep one step ahead, not wanting to lose the advantage.

"Carmela." She dropped the word without turning her head.

"That's a lovely name ..."

"Nothing special, thousands of girls in this country are called Carmela."

"Maybe. But the owner of the name is very special: a very attractive and intelligent woman."

I knew how awkward my compliments sounded and got embarrassed, becoming aware of my unprepossessing appearance, of my uncovered bald pate. (I'd forgotten my hat in the hotel.) I touched my chin: a three-day stubble only increased my shyness.

Carmela stopped walking and looked straight into my face:

"So you like me, eh?!" she smiled.

I felt relieved. The ice between us was broken.

"Would you care to have a drink somewhere along the beach?"

"Sure," she said simply, as if expecting to be invited.

It was getting dark quickly and the stars were already out. I looked up, but couldn't recognize the familiar constellations: they seemed to be at the wrong angle. The moon, like an overturned beetle, was lying belly up. The tables of a restaurant-bar were placed near the water, their feet sinking in the sand. We took the one nearest to the tideline.

A dark-skinned, Indian-looking waiter brought the menu, placed some glasses, and stabilized the shaky table.

Then he put his arm around Carmela and kissed her on each cheek the way Mexicans greet each other. I opened the menu, counting on Carmela's help.

"Oh, Carmelita, sweetheart! Where have you been? We were looking for you everywhere!" came from a table next to ours. Three or four men sitting there seemed to be quite loaded. One of them made an attempt, with some theatrical flourish, to move from his table to ours, but couldn't disengage his dangling Frankenstein frame from the chair which was sinking deeper into the sand the more he struggled. His two pals were egging him on.

"C'mon, one more time, just lift your ass!"

"Stay put, Bob, don't you dare move!" shouted Carmela in English, waving a 'no' to the man. " ," she turned to the waiter: "Go, talk to him."

"*De acuerdo,*" said Francisco, parting his gelled hair with a quick movement of both hands.

I turned to Carmela. "Everybody seems to know you here."

"Sure. I come here every summer. See the white house on the bluff? That's my studio."

Carmela pointed towards the ocean, across the bay, but I couldn't see anything in the darkness.

"By the way, these three are also from Canada. They sleep by day, crawl out of their burrows at night and get drunk like pigs."

"How do you know them?"

"The tall one, Bob, was my model."

"He looks like a complete waste. Is he always loaded like that?" I said.

"I don't really care. He is a picturesque type, that's all I want. Look at his head, his wide, heavy jaw; look how his face narrows towards his forehead, a rare bone arrangement. He told me he is a *mestizo*, half Indian, half Norwegian."

"We call them Métis. First Nations people mixed with Whites."

"That's like our descendants of Spanish and Indians then. He is fighting for the rights of his people, he said, and he is obsessed with diamonds. He even gave me one," she touched the pendulum on her neck.

"That's a generous gift!" I grinned.

"He got his portrait in exchange, didn't he? He had nothing to pay with and I'm expensive."

"Where is he from, you said?" I was a little baffled by all this.

"Somewhere from the North, some kind of a knife..." Carmela shook her hand in the air.

"Yellowknife," I said. "It's true, they did find lots of diamonds there recently. The Métis consider the land theirs and want some share in it together with the Dené Indians; there's a dispute, you see. But the Dené don't recognize the Métis. They are not 'Indian' enough for them, and for the Whites, they are not really Whites. The Métis are falling into the crack between, neither here, nor there."

"A hard place to be!" said Carmela looking at the candle on the table whose reflected light danced in her squinting eyes. I couldn't get rid of the feeling that her remark was aimed at me rather than the fat Métis at the next table. But then I felt so unsure of myself in the presence of this woman.

I tried to explain something about Canadian policy towards the First Nations.

"What's the First Nations, anyway? Funny name."

A stray dog came up and rubbed against Carmela's chair, then looked at her with pleading eyes. The scruffy creature had separated from the pack and was hunting for the leftovers at the beach joints on its own. Carmela made an abrupt movement to scare the dog off, got up and started to readjust her chair. I could see she was quickly losing interest in my rhetoric.

"So you're a painter," I tried to change the subject. "That's interesting. I know there is a rich art tradition in Mexico. What style do you work in?"

Carmela gave me a quick contemptuous look.

"I'm sorry, I know little about painting. I mean, is it abstractionism or surrealism, or perhaps…"

Embarrassingly, I was running out of words for styles and she certainly wasn't helping me.

"I paint lungs and vaginas," said Carmela calmly.

"I beg your pardon?"

"Not human lungs, though. The vaginas are human all right, but the lungs are from sheep. I take sheep lungs, I dry them out. You know what they look like when dry?" She was now truly animated. "Like small white balloons, sausage-shaped. And then I attach them to the painted surfaces. I have one piece in the Museum of Contemporary Art in Mexico City. You've been there? Perhaps you noticed the painted blue sky with clouds over the entrance arch. They look like painted clouds, but in fact, it's sheep lungs."

I didn't know exactly how to react, so I nodded and smiled, just in case.

The waiter brought the *sangría* I had ordered for Carmela. He'd obviously heard our conversation.

"She is famous, sir! Everybody knows her here and even in Mexico City," he said in his heavily accented English.

"Oh, shut up Paco!" Carmela snapped.

"*Poco tímida, poco dispuesta.* It is true, what I said. You go to a big museum, she is there, like Rivera," Francisco patted Carmela on the shoulder.

"Hey, chum! Get your hands off her! Better bring us another beer!" shouted Bob, the Métis, across the table. Then he made yet another attempt to disengage himself from the chair.

Carmela said something to the waiter in Spanish, and he went over to the table where Bob sat with his half-drunk pals.

"If you wish to see my work, you can come to my studio," said Carmela softly.

Alone in my hotel room, I couldn't stop thinking about her: the way she tossed her hair, the way her long slim arms danced as she talked. She had this habit of turning her head away in the middle of the conversation as if gazing at something only she could see. But her eyes remained strangely still, both searching for something, yet indifferent to what they found. Her eyes watched you, but kept what they observed hidden.

2

Carmela's cottage was perched on top of the bluff over-looking the ocean, and I had to climb up the winding stairs, cut in the solid rock to reach abundant bougainvil-lea camouflaging the entrance to her studio. The door was ajar when I stepped into an unusual space of movable canvas partitions, positioned at different angles to each other. Between them the fresh breeze from the ocean wandered freely. The partitions looked like sails and were perfect for exhibiting art. One wall of the studio was all glass and through it down below I could see waves beating against the rocks, and above them, the horizon. I felt I was drifting through shimmering azure that was both the ocean and the sky.

At first, I didn't recognize Carmela: her long hair was tired up in a bun at the back, exposing her long neck. But her dry, businesslike manner contrasted with her attire: when she stood against the light, her diaphanous Turkish *chalivari* exposed her legs to the thighs. She was wearing the same diamond pendulum I saw on her when I met her on the beach.

'Have a look at my work,' she said, pointing to some elaborate frames leaning against the wall.

"This was commissioned by the Museum of Modern Art in Mexico City. I need to make three more pieces."

I looked for paintings inside the frames, but found none. Instead, there were fabrics of different textures and colors, mostly in red hues: from scarlet velvet, to pink silk. The material was collected in folds to form in the centre of each frame an ovoid shape. "*Retratos de familia*," said the sign.

"Do you like it?"

I removed my sunglasses in order to see better, but they

slipped out of my fingers. As I bent down to pick them up, blood rushed to my head and I had to sit on my haunches for a minute waiting for the fiery circles behind my eyelids to stop their clockwork prance. Carmela silently watched me.

"Oh, yes, they are quite unusual," I said finally getting up and catching my breath.

"Do you like them, though? Well, you don't have to. Come, what do you think of those?"

She moved over to three identical objects perched on high stools. They looked like leather purses with metal buckles.

"Just look inside them."

I opened one purse and instinctively shut it back. Unabashed, I was staring inside the female genitalia meticulously reproduced in pink leather.

"I came up with this idea and somehow it caught on. I have a rich client who wants ten of those. I can't fathom what for." Carmela chuckled.

I imagined this woman spending her days readjusting the wrinkles, adding a little bit here, taking away there … I was instantly embarrassed by this thought and looked sideways. My glance fell on small statuettes on a low shelf in the corner.

One of them was a Mexican God with the face of a jaguar and an elaborate hairdress. Painted blood was dripping from both sides of his mouth. The other figure was a sitting man: one part of him flesh, the other, skeleton.

"These are replicas," explained Carmela. "The originals are in the Anthropological Museum in Mexico City."

"I hadn't realized before I went to that museum," I said, "to what degree the whole culture was based on premeditated slaughter. When I first saw all this art collected in one place, I was truly repulsed."

"Magnificent artisans, though," said Carmela, turning the skeleton-man in her hands. "Yes, it is morbid, I agree. But life is morbid – it contains death. They didn't deny the reality, that's all. Aren't we all walking skeletons, after all? Just waiting for the external layer of the deception to fall off?" she smiled with that familiar whimsical smile of hers.

"One way of looking at it, I suppose. I spent two days in this museum and I now have a hard time blaming Cortez for his cruelty. There was a statuette of a man wearing human skin on top of his own. Then these games … I didn't realize that even their games were a ritualized murder. *Palata* or *peleta*, I'm not sure."

"*Pelota*."

"All right, *pelota*. But you know what I'm talking about, don't your? If, by mistake, the ball ended up flying counter the sun's movement, the whole team would lose their heads. Then they would pile those heads on the central city square. Imagine Aztec children passing by decomposing heads every day. "

"Death can be beautiful," said Carmela and smiled again.

"Yes, but every time I'll find myself on the *Zócalo* now, I am going to think about these heads. See, I respect the culture, the tradition. I know these were their beliefs, but the scope of it we simply fail to ..."

We were interrupted by a knock at the door. Francisco stood on the porch staring at me. Obviously, he didn't expect to see me.

"Sorry, sir," he said.

"I'm busy now, Paco,"Carmela said, and I could feel her irritation. "We're working, Joseph and I. He is going to sit for my portrait. You can come and clean up later. By the way, did you get me some solvent?"

Francisco took a bottle out of his pocket and placed it on the table.

"That's good. Thank you. So, around four or five then, not before."

"*Entiendo,*" responded Francisco, softly closing the door behind him.

"I didn't realize, you wanted to paint my portrait," I said to Carmela.

"Of course, I do. I'm always looking out for new models. You can only do that many vaginas. Usually people don't say 'no' to me. Everybody wants to have their image immortalized, but the problem is I don't want to paint just anybody. I will only charge you half price. After my death, your portrait will be worth a fortune. You'll make money on me if you ever decide to sell it."

I was taken aback by her intention to sell me something I didn't ask for. But even more bizarre was the casual way she mentioned her own death, as if she was talking about a complete stranger and more than that, she knew exactly when this stranger was going to die. Perhaps death was as much part of her culture as ignoring it was part of mine.

"You have an interesting face. Quite asymmetrical. I like that. Can you sit for the next twenty minutes without moving at all?"

She positioned me in a chair, then stepped back to her easel, gazing at me intently.

"Tilt your head a little forward, please. That's too much. No, just the way it was before."

"I don't remember how it was before."

She walked over to me, took my head in both her hands and angled it slightly forward, then stepped back to her easel.

"Now you've lifted it again."

"Did I? Should it be like this?"

"No. That's still too much. Don't bring your head so far back. Gives you an air of arrogance. Which is not in your nature."

I was bemused by her perceptiveness. It was only the second time she'd seen me.

"Sit naturally. Relax. And now take off your shirt." I

didn't move. Did I misunderstand her?

"Undress. Down to your waist." It was an order, not a request.

"I thought you were going to paint my portrait; mostly, my face ... "

She didn't respond and continued to paint.

When I awkwardly pulled my shirt up, her eyes glided over me, taking me all in. It was a quick evaluating look, both intense and indifferent at the same time. I was no more than an object in space, a form that reflected and absorbed light in a certain manner. Sweat rolled down my armpits. I became painfully aware of dark flabby patches of skin under my armpits; of my grey bushy breasts softened and enlarged by age. I was embarrassed and hunched instinctively, hiding my chest, but then there were my hands: old, knotty and dark against my pale protruded belly. Time has plowed and plundered my body and I couldn't hide its debris from the young woman so mercilessly and coldly scrutinizing it.

My forehead was soaking wet with tension. Carmela noticed it and handed me a piece of white cloth. Then, with a quick automatic movement, as if unaware of what she was doing, she pulled up her own blouse.

Taken by surprise, I made an involuntary sound. Her breasts were perfectly shaped, though unexpectedly heavy for her slender body. They were lighter olive than the rest of her skin. But her nipples were dark, with large dark aureolas around them. I forced myself to look away. Carmela, on the contrary, showed no sign of discomfort – as if stripping in front of a stranger was a very ordinary thing for her.

"Don't move. I need you to look outside yourself, not inside. Focus on something that interests you," said Carmela. "That's why I've undressed."

She started painting again, moving from easel to palette, adding some brush strokes and then stepping away from the canvas. I couldn't but follow each of her movements: the way her breasts sagged forward as she bent over, and then lifted up as she reached for the upper corner of the canvas, swayed as she turned.

The sight of her nakedness transported me to a hot and humid afternoon of my childhood, half a century ago, my mother, still young, firmly clasping my steaming hand as she pushed her way through a crowd of women surrounding the tables with heaps of discount clothes in the basement of a second-hand store in Toronto. I must have been nine or ten then and I remember black women's torsos brushing against my cheek, the sickening, foetid smell of unwashed flesh … And then – the crackling of static: I was almost blinded, both repulsed and drawn to what I saw: folds of flesh brimming over and under brassieres as women quickly removed their tops in front of my eyes, pulling over their half-naked bodies sweaters and blouses they'd snatched from the tables. I panicked and tried to run away, but my mother held firmly to my hand, afraid to lose me in the crowd. And then I saw a young mulatto girl, not older than myself, with the long angular body of a boy. She too took off her top, but to my surprise, there was nothing under it, except for two round, well-formed spheres, lighter in color than the rest of her body, two alert dark-eyed creatures living a separate life on her small frame. I stared at the girl, transfixed. I was overpowered by a strange sensation: it was the first awakening of desire, but mostly, it was a deep longing for something elusive that I knew even then as I know now would always be out of my reach.

"Talk to me, it helps my work," said Carmela.

"What shall we talk about?" I cleared up my throat trying to regain my normal voice.

"Yourself … When people talk of themselves, they are never bored or tired. They come to life and that's exactly what I want in a portrait. Where are you from?"

"I was born in Toronto, but then we moved to Winnipeg." She didn't react. I'm sure she'd never heard of the place.

"Are you a businessman?"

"Why, do I look like one?"

"You can never tell with foreigners. Some of them look like beggars on the beach, then you find out they are famous poets."

"If I tell you I'm a poet, will you make me look

handsome?"

"You are handsome. Very much so."

I found it hard to believe her. Her measuring eyes moved from me to the canvas and back in rapid succession. She wasn't really interested in me – again I became acutely aware of that – other than as a pictorial object.

"Well, I'm not a businessman, but my father was. He owned a factory in China. Made a fortune manufacturing plastic bags."

I don't know why I told her about my father. Did I intuitively sense that some genetic connection with money and success would make me more attractive in her eyes?

"Boring, no?"

"What's boring?"

"Manufacturing bags."

"Not if it brings you lots of money!"

"You sound like an American."

She came up to me, touched my shoulders and tilted my head. Her naked breasts lightly brushed against my forearm. I lost my train of thought.

"Have you ever been to China? I've always wanted to go … " she asked.

"Oh, a long time ago. I was twenty then. My father hoped I would enter the family business and decided I had to see his factory. I met with his employees, Chinese girls, over a hundred of them, aged from sixteen to twenty-five. They lived in a dorm, seven girls per room. My father didn't want them to commute to work."

"Your father was an exploiter, then?"

"No, he paid his workers well. Twenty-five per cent more than anywhere else in China. He was a good man, but I still didn't want to become a businessman."

She put her brushes down and began to smudge paint on the canvas with her finger.

"Money makes life easier. Lots of money, I mean."

"I have never been rich myself. But when my father died, things changed..."

I was getting uncomfortable with the subject.

"Well now, it's your turn to tell me about yourself," I said.

"What is it you want to know?" Carmela held up the stem of a brush against her outstretched hand, measuring the proportions of my body; then she moved it to the canvas, comparing.

"Your friend, the waiter, said you're already a well-known artist. Yet you're so young."

"Who said that, Francisco? It's true, he admires me. But he knows nothing about art. He is a handyman; makes frames for my pictures. Very good with his hands, but he believes I'll go straight to hell for my pussy bags!"

Laughter overcame her, she put her brush down.

"Oh, look what I did to myself!" She cupped her left breast into her hands and tried to remove the yellowish stain from around the nipple with her finger. The stain smudged.

She came up to me still holding her breast absently in her hand. I felt intimidated.

"Can you lift your head again? Do not tilt it. Just keep it steady. That's it. And stop worrying about your hands. I'm not working on them right now … "

I held my breath, I was so tense. But she stepped back, releasing the yellow-daubed breast just as absently, and I felt somewhat relieved.

"It's true, I lucked out. Had several exhibitions in London as a student, and after that got a green light at home. They love it when the foreign press talks about you."

"Your parents must have given you a good jump-start in life," I said.

"My parents?" She smirked and rubbed something on her canvas with a piece of cloth. "My father I hardly knew. He was traveling when I was a child, and he still is. My mother? She liked to read a lot. Thought it was a waste of time to spend the night sleeping. An insomniac. She was half-asleep most of the time during the day though. I remember I'd ask her a question and she'd look at me, and I knew she hadn't heard. She lives in Paris now."

Carmela fell silent. She glanced at me at a rarer intervals now, absorbed more with her creation than with the original. Finally, she declared the session over, faced the picture to the wall – it wasn't finished yet – and cleaned her hands with the solvent. I couldn't tell if she was happy with her work or not.

I felt tired. I hadn't realized how difficult it was to sit without motion. All the time I was aware of her nakedness and my own decaying flesh, and that made me even more tense. I closed my eyes for a moment, but was startled out of my torpor by a light touch on my check. I opened my eyes – Carmela quickly and lithely sat on my lap. The weight of her body and the coolness of her stroking fingers on my face were so unexpected that I felt limp, almost paralyzed, but Carmela pressed her naked breast against my cheek and forced her nipple into my mouth.

"Lick that stain off, would you?" she whispered, rising, drawing me with her, maneuvering me to the sofa.

I finally gave myself up to her body. She exhausted me in what somehow seemed a vengeful, yet delightful delirium, and then I lay there, listening to the waves lapping the rocks at the foot of her house. I listened to the shrieks of the albatrosses; to the subdued shouts of dark-skinned boys selling coconuts; and then my mind moved further away, drifting over her ancient and arid land that lay in wait around us with its enigmatic pyramids and the dead cities, long abandoned by priests and gods, who had sated themselves on human blood; and somehow Carmela herself was this ancient land strewn with cacti; she was the orange flames of the sunset and the endless sky. She was a high priest ready for the sacrifice, and the innocent girl being sacrificed. The blood of both, the executioner and the victim, ran in her veins.

And then I looked at her, curled in the crook of my arm which had started to go to sleep under the weight of her head, and was struck by her innocent look. Her cheeks were flushed, mouth slightly open, and all the predatory vigor, all the insatiability that had stormed inside her only minutes ago was gone. The arrogance and the aloofness that she had put between herself and the world disappeared. Here was a young woman, almost a girl, in her most natural and beautiful state. Never before did I feel such rapture and yet such tenderness for any human being. Her clean forehead was like a prism that collected in its focus all my love, all my tenderness, all my old longings. She was everything I had never had: my lover, my daughter, my sister, my wife. The more I looked at her, in that deep repose, the less I could imagine having made love to her, having actually penetrated her – so crude seemed now any such desire compared to the feelings brimming over my soul, feelings for which I had no name.

I had no doubt that Fate had entrusted her to my care. The world was a sleepwalker wandering around with eyes half closed: now I had to protect her against this world. I imagined myself to be her self-appointed knight in whose presence, finally, perhaps for the first time in her life, she would be able to remove her mask and breathe freely.

My daydreaming was disrupted by a sudden noise. In our bliss, we had completely forgotten about Francisco, who had half-opened the unlocked front door. Carmela grabbed a sheet from the bed, wrapped herself up and went to meet Francisco.

I, a little shaky on my legs, carried my over-pouring heart down the winding stairs into a freshly painted, festive and ever so gentle world.

3

What were the days that followed that magic afternoon like? I couldn't tell you: patches of morning light drifting from the water to the palm trees to Carmela's hair, as she was combing it after a swim; the unhurried movement of her hand; the ocean, the breeze, the sand, hot at noon, slowly cooling after the sunset, the distillation of my perfect happiness, my bliss – that's all I remember. The nights fell upon us suddenly, and the granular light of stars, as if seen for the first time, filled me with fresh awe. They were my witnesses and I thought that my love for Carmela was as uncanny as the light of these stars, created for us and us alone.

Sometimes, returning to my hotel from the cottage of High Sails (that's what I came to call her little studio on the bluff), I asked myself whether I was daydreaming, or simply losing my wits: how could a young, exquisitely beautiful and talented woman fall for an utterly banal old man like myself? But the moment she put her lovely arm around me or looked at me, all my doubts would evaporate and, I, covering the velvety inside of her arm with kisses all the way up to a slightly wet, acid armpit, would be instantly thrown into euphoria and feel that somehow I deserved her love, deserved that happiness.

I wanted to be with her all the time, but felt a teenaged shyness in her presence: I was afraid to touch her, but she always took the initiative, relieving me of my fears. She made love to me passionately, with abandon – and that gave me confidence I never experienced before: I was wanted, even desired, in spite of my age and unassuming appearance. All of it was new to me and I gradually began to see myself in a different light. To think of it, I wasn't that old. And weren't the wrinkles, after all, the external expression of accumulated wisdom? No wonder many women found older men attractive. As for the folds of skin hanging from under my chin, when I looked at myself in profile, in dim bathroom light, I could easily see the resemblance to some noble aging Roman Senator, if not Julius Caesar himself.

There were also delightful moments of what she called "domestic coziness". And they, more than intense passion, convinced me of her affection for me. I could see that she, too, needed me, perhaps even loved me.

My utter inability to draw amused her. Sitting next to me, she loved to guide my fingers, awkwardly squeezing the pencil, over the paper. I laughed in disbelief when all of a sudden, out of nothing, emerged a cat climbing a tree, a hunchbacked woman sitting sideways on a chair, an Indian boy carving something with a knife. She started teaching me Spanish with a patience that I didn't expect from her. When I asked her once why my knowing her language was important to her, she said that it would make her feel closer to me. I was enthralled. I repeated the sounds of her tongue that I grew to love as mantra, as token of our union.

Every morning I continued to sit for my portrait; then we would have a light snack and go down to the beach with two big towels and a basket of fruit. I was sporting white linen pants and a loose, colorfully embroidered shirt that she bought for me from the local artisans; she had a yellow, wide-skirted sundress and a straw hat with a wide brim that suited her dark complexion so well.

Having grown up inland, I didn't understand the ocean, but Carmela was an excellent and fearless swimmer. Nevertheless, every time her dark head disappeared in the surging green precipices, my heart sank. I felt it was I at the mercy of the waves, for she now became part of me.

"Ask the ocean to throw you the key and then enter," she shouted between her dives, playing with the waves and my fear. The breakers were high, and I stood there helpless, watching her.

She taught me to count waves: while the tallest, the seventh wave, was amassing its strength and then smashing into the beach, I had to run into the ocean as fast as I could, and swim out. "That's the only way the ocean will let you in," she shouted, "on the seventh wave."

Often, we were the only ones who ventured into the stormy surf, the locals sitting on the beach watching us. What a joy it was after the frantic paddling to finally reach calmer waters beyond the raging surf, turn around and watch the ocean thrust with its flagellating power onto the beach. I would try to keep up with Carmela's quick crawl and hug her in the water, but she would slip out and swim away.

One day she told me she had to leave the beach earlier – a reporter was waiting for her in the studio.

"What reporter?" I tried not to sound alarmed. Her dealings with men, particularly strangers, whom I couldn't know, made me a little nervous. But I didn't want to acknowledge even to myself that these tinkling needles in my brain were the first signs of jealousy. "A journalist from the local radio station," said Carmela, pulling her sundress on top of a wet swimming suit. "I completely forgot. He's going to run a preview of my September show."

She was in a visible rush now. I helped her stick the wet towels into the canvas bag. "I'll carry it," I said. "I'm going to walk you to the cottage anyway."

"Oh, that's all right. I can carry it myself." Carmela turned and looked at me. "You know what I'd like to do?"

"What?"

"Guess?" She smiled conspiratorially. "After this interview, I'd like to come to your hotel and stay overnight. I'll be wearing this special dress and I'll pretend I don't know you and then ... " She whispered something into my ear, then burst into laughter.

Lately, I had noticed a playful side in her that wasn't there before – and I loved it. I lifted her in my arms, overwhelmed with joy. The prospect of spending an entire night with her immediately reconciled me to the impending separation.

At the cottage of High Sails I kissed her good-bye and began to climb up the hill back to my hotel. The sun was getting very hot, and I thought I should take a nap to replenish my energy before her arrival later that evening. I almost made it to the hotel, when I noticed that I was missing my wristwatch. It must have slipped into the sand somehow and I hadn't noticed. Annoyed at myself – now I had to go all the way back to the beach – I reluctantly turned around.

The terrain sloped to the ocean and I saw Carmela from afar. She was on the same spot we both had left ten minutes ago, lying in the arms of a man, her legs wrapped around his torso. Not quite trusting my own eyes, I stopped, then slowly moved forward. I couldn't see the man's face, but I recognized him from the back: it was Francisco. I felt that the world, as I knew it, was vanishing – or rather, the world was still there, but I was no longer able to grasp its meaning: everything around me became drained of vibrancy: the sky seemed monotonously blue, the sand, dull yellow. I stood there, still seeing and yet not being able to see, a dull drone in my ears. Then I moved forward as if still hoping the mirage would disperse. When Francisco got up, I noticed how muscular his legs were. I stared at his hairy calves and thighs that seemed to threaten me and be the focus of my pain. Francisco hopped twice, balancing on one foot while pulling a pant leg over the other. Then he sat down next to Carmela, and she put her arm around him, reaching for her bag with the other hand. She took out some grapes we had brought to the beach, inserted one grape into her own mouth, then took Francisco's head into her hands and pushed it into his mouth with her tongue – her favourite game – the way she had done with me so many times. At the beginning the man was passive, but then they both broke into laughter. He pretended to move away from her but she found his mouth again and they kissed.

I turned around and went back to the hotel.

Without removing my shoes, I collapsed on my bed and covered my head with a sheet. I didn't have any thoughts or feelings. It was late afternoon and the hotel was filled with sounds: people in the hallway were talking loudly in Spanish; somebody was taking a shower, then there was the erratic noise of running feet, must be children. I lay there listening through the sheet, waiting for night to fall. I still hoped for one and one sound only: her light, hesitant tap on my door. What would I do then? Pretend I didn't know anything and forgive her? My heart turned painfully in my chest. No, I won't humiliate myself with explanations. I will simply leave the room without as much as a word or a touch. I'll get out of the country as soon as possible – and then from a plane I'll write her a brief letter. She will regret what she had done, but it will be too late.

I raised myself to look at the time, but then remembered that I had left my watch on the beach. I must have spent hours in bed, for now it was completely dark. No sounds were coming from the corridor. I realized in an instant that Carmela was not going to come because she was spending the night with Francisco. Though I could imagine her making love to another man, my mind refused to believe it, as if it was somehow against the laws of nature and therefore couldn't be happening to me. That night I was unable to get any sleep at all. One moment I wanted to inflict pain on her, so that she would know all the measure of my suffering; the next, I wanted to forgive her; for some strange reason, I even felt sorry for her. I was sweating profusely. Then I started coughing. Unable to contain my fits anymore, I finally got up and went out for some fresh air. In the hallway, a short blonde woman was leaning against the wall, one barefoot leg rubbing the other. The moment she saw me, she snuck her feet into stiletto shoes standing beside her. She watched me struggling with my cough for a while, then unglued herself from the wall and began to twist her foot inside the shoe, rotating her hips in sync with her movements.

"Fucking sand!" she said, balancing on one foot and emptying her left shoe out.

"Do you know where the laundry is?" She spoke in a raspy voice with the deep drawl of a Southerner.

"Pardon? The laundry? Sorry, I don't."

"I mean, where do you do your washing?" She emptied her second shoe. "I don't know anybody in this place. Would you like to spend the evening together?"

I looked at her more carefully: bleached hair, a nondescript faded face, a rather plump figure. She looked grubby, second-hand, yet her body had a not unpleasant roundedness about it.

"It must be very late now. What time is it?" I said hesitatingly.

"I know a very good restaurant not far from here," she said without responding to my question. "They are open till midnight. The owner says his great-grandfather invented Caesar salad a century ago at that place, and they still serve it the old way there."

I lifted my eyebrows in disbelief but agreed to accompany her. Her face lit up.

"Before spending a pleasant evening in the company of such a nice gentleman, I need to have my pedicure done, hope you don't mind." She moved closer to me and I smelled her cheap perfume.

Ten minutes later, we were entering a suspicious-looking den, with several billiard tables and phone booths at the front. A barbershop was somewhere in the back. My companion said something in labored Spanish to a woman with an apron and pink curls on her head. The woman brought out a copper basin filled with water and placed it on a low stool. With one foot in the basin, the other stretched out in the lap of the pedicurist, my new acquaintance winked at me: "We should get to know each other better. I've had an interesting life, if you are curious."

I said I was, and she embarked on a story that sounded so grotesque that I immediately recognized a fellow tall-tales teller, a kindred spirit of sorts, wondering all along if making up this nonsense was her way of supplementing her other, much more dubious, yet lucrative source of income, or if she did it for pure pleasure – her own and that of a prospective client.

If I were to believe her, she was an orphan, raised by her grandfather, who took her as a lover at the tender age of thirteen, and then, in an act of repentance, married her off to his wealthy friend over sixty; his intentions being good, he was unable, however, to restrain his obsession with his granddaughter and continued to demand her favors. It resulted in a ménage à trois that ended tragically: the granddaughter finally poisoned the grandfather, freeing herself from the terrible double bondage; at the same time, she doomed herself to the life of a perpetual vagabond.

"If they find me, I'm finished," said the woman, abruptly slashing the air in front of her throat. Her fear of men was so engraved in her ever since, she added, that she would never think of going to bed before barricading her door first.

Life can be stranger than fiction, they say, but whether there was any truth in her concoction or not, for me her story had one indisputable merit: it distracted me from my own pain. Yet, I was quickly getting weary. I paid for the woman's pedicure and was prepared to return to the hotel, when she reminded me I had promised to take her to a restaurant. She was going to take a shower, could I wait a minute in the lobby?

I reluctantly agreed, but forty minutes later I was still there waiting for her. Finally, feeling exhausted and fooled, I knocked at her door. There was an unmistakable sound of furniture being moved around, then the door opened just enough for me to see a pile of chairs atop each other and a naked arm handed over to me as if for a kiss. I didn't quite know what to do with this hand, but while I was hesitating, the door slammed in my face. I heard the furniture being moved back in place. I knocked again, but was both annoyed and relieved not to receive any answer.

I don't remember how I survived till the next day, but by late afternoon I couldn't take it anymore and found myself at the door of Carmela's studio.

"Come on in, Joe," she smiled at me as if nothing at all had happened.

"I didn't sleep last night … I was waiting for you," I said, half-averting my face. "I know what has happened, I know where you've been." I tried to sound as calm as possible.

"You mean the interview? I was too tired to come to your hotel after the interview. It dragged on and on," said Carmela, turned around and walked into her studio.

"You don't need to lie to me, Carmela," I said following her. "I saw you with Francisco on the beach."

"So what?" She turned to me, her eyes squinting. "Can't I talk to another man? What would you like to drink? I have some freshly squeezed mango." She opened the fridge.

"No, thanks. But let's not get off the subject. Why didn't you tell me you had a lover all along? Instead of telling me that he made frames for you and so on. Why lie?"

"What I said was true." Carmela calmly poured herself some juice. "He does make frames for me. He even helped

me to build this studio." I noticed the mist gathering on
the inside surface of her glass. I felt sudden indifference
to everything, but my senses seemed to live lives of their
own, noticing everything, infusing every trifle with an
annoying significance.

"And that's why you slept with him?"

"Don't you dare insult me!" Carmela suddenly
exploded and slammed her glass onto the countertop.
Juice poured over the counter, glass smatterings bursting
in all directions. I watched one piece rocking behind the
leg of a chair, its amplitude of motion smaller and smaller.
Her sudden rage took me by surprise, but I noticed that
her eyes remained cold as usual.

"Yes, he is my lover, and you knew all the time about
us and chose to accept it!"

I was appalled at how quickly she had abandoned
all her pretence and even the smallest effort to spare me
the truth! Had she invented some semi-plausible story,
I would have grabbed onto it and lamely, torturously
believed her.

"I just want to know one thing. Why did you start an
affair with me when all that time you had another lover?"

I felt a sudden urge to relieve myself. I ran to the toilet
but stopped short in front of the image staring at me out
of the mirror: bulging eyes surrounded by deep furrows,
the helpless grimace of a weak, drooping mouth and the
long, vertical lines crossing my cheeks all the way down

to my neck. There was no way, simply no way, that I, Joseph Parson, sixty years old, could legitimately defend the claims of this monkey in front of that young woman full of life and vigor!

I came out of the bathroom. Carmela was applying some lotion to her face, the way she often did before going to the beach, and when I saw that familiar gesture, the helpless ugly ape that had stared at me a minute ago from a bathroom mirror, and with whose behavior I had nothing in common, suddenly dropped on its knees in front of her, grabbed her legs, wept uncontrollably.

"Forgive me," I sobbed, "Forgive me! I didn't want to hurt you!"

"Why are you so upset?" said Carmela, looking down at me. "It's just sex."

"I thought that you and I ... that you loved me a little too; you can't love me the way I love you, I know that, but I hoped that ... " My vocal cords gave up, the sound of my voice thinning into a whisper.

"Well, I like you all right! You're somehow different, and your stories are funny. Francisco is a bore compared to you. He is a waiter, a handyman; he does my errands, for God's sake! How can you be jealous of him? Calm down, *querido. No hay que ahogarse en un vaso de agua.* You don't have to drown in a glass of water!"

A hopeless despair overcame me: I was enraged and words came back to me, gushing out of my mouth uncontrollably, without my will.

"So you sleep with everybody whom you find funny, or whom you can boss around and treat like your slave! What about that guy, whatever his name, that drunkard who gave you a diamond? You slept with him too, didn't you?"

"What business is that of yours? I am a free woman."

She took another glass from the dish rack, poured herself some juice, gulped it down and wiped her mouth with the back of her hand.

"After all, we are not married; you can't tell me what to do!"

"You mean if you were my wife, it would make a difference?"

"Oh, sure. Then you could have as much of me as you wished and Francisco would be our handyman, our gardener. He would look after our house for cheap." She paused. "He'd make more frames for my cunts. What do you think?"

For the first time in my life I was about to hit a woman. But I restrained myself. I got up and quickly left, determined never to see her again.

4

Next day I started planning my return to Canada. Looking back at recent events I saw clearly that Carmela wasn't at all whom I had taken her to be. An imposter with philistine pretensions using art to lure men into bed; a nymphomaniac, manufacturing pussy bags – that's all she was! The more I thought about her, the more my own delusions became painfully obvious to me. I became convinced that she didn't have as much as a spark of artistic talent in her. How then could she have drawn me into all this, making me sit for her for a whole month? Was I completely blind? I had anticipated sessions with her with such impatience! The mere sight of bougainvillea camouflaging the door that led into her world had sent my heart into reverential leaps. Her sleepy whisper in the morning when the first rays of the sun set her ebon hair on fire, that innocent whisper in my half-alert ear made me believe she was a fragile flower in need of my protection, whereas in fact she was cynical and hard as stones and I was an old fool, doting over a predator who toyed with me, her prey, before destroying it.

The memories of nights made for our love now existed solely for my torment. Anger, shame and the old, still unquenched desire for her inundated me at night: I was out of breath, I was suffocating. The sheets felt wet against

my exhausted body. My tortured ear would shut out the
drone of the fan only to yield to the cadenced rage of the
ocean below that was smashing itself against the sand
strewn with dead crabs and empty shells. What was this
ocean raging against? The limits imposed by its shores?
How pointless, how futile.

Yesterday I spotted decomposing white flesh on the
sand. I thought it was a dead dog, but it turned out to
be a huge turtle without its shell, its pale sinewy tissue
exposed to the sun. The ocean burped it out, then left it
there to rot.

In the time that followed, I tried not to think of Carmela. But I soon discovered that it was impossible, and the
harder I tried, the less I succeeded. My resolve to return
immediately to Canada faded into ennui. Slowly, my anger gave place to a dull pain that nestled inside my heart
and that I couldn't either pull out or ignore. I couldn't hate
her – hating her meant hating myself. But no matter what
I did, I was hurting as if I had lost something vital for my
existence – a pair of limbs – yet was forced to drag my
body through the desert of smiling strangers, pretend-
ing that I, just like them, was whole. I knew I couldn't
grow new limbs any more than I would be able to love
somebody else in what remained of my life. I felt more
and more isolated from the world and gradually sank into

the realm of dreams that alone seemed to be bringing me some relief. At dawn I would go into slumber and watch the misshapen fragments of my thoughts (ragged little Daliesque creatures) floating inside my brain. I'd try to pull one out and hold on to it before it dissipated. One rectangular shape took the form of a coffin – at closer inspection, my own. I couldn't clearly see my face inside it: my white sunken cheeks were camouflaged with some quivering shadows of leaves that the trees obligingly lent me. The coffin was drawn by a horse which knew where to go. Nobody followed the procession. My death seemed to be exactly like each of my birthdays, a lonely and redundant affair. Self-pity overwhelmed me and I cried in my sleep. Then I woke up, flipped aside the gauze hanging from the ceiling. I couldn't stand being enclosed in a coffin, a swaddled larva, a mummy, a corpse! I made an effort to get up but my resolve quickly evaporated and imperceptibly I was drifting into another dream. This one shimmered with the glory and sweetness of happiness, as Carmela, my beloved, returned to me as a very young girl, almost a child, whom I had known all my life. In my dream she was not my mistress, but my wife of many years. We were the same age; we grew up together, married, became old, and then came full circle and regained our youth. Around us, the water was lapping gently, our bed drifting away into the warm, milky abyss. Carmela was both delighted and scared. "Don't leave me," she said, "I've forgotten how to swim." "Are you afraid, my sweet? Nothing is gentler than water. I will protect you. I will go anywhere you go."

I woke up and knew I wasn't alone any more: imagining I could preserve the aura of her presence, her smell and her warmth, I skipped my shower for two days. That dream was a turning point in my life: it made me postpone my return home, for now I had an urgent task to complete. I had to secure her new glorious existence inside me: not only should the malice of the outside world be unable to touch her, but she should be beyond the reach of my own anger, my own jealousy lest they destroy her shining image. I kept listening to the new music that was enveloping my soul with such tenderness. In a strange fashion, we reversed our roles; now she became my guardian angel protecting me from slipping into darkness. How that transformation happened, I don't know. I think it was akin to *satori,* the awakening of the heart, allowing you to see the true nature of the world. That sensation could not have been inferred from any events that had preceded it. Yet it was irreversible. It was then that I forgave her and forgave myself for wanting her all for myself and hating her if she didn't belong to me alone. That forgiveness gave new freedom to my spirit and strength to my body. The world around me was bathing in a warm light of mercy. Now I didn't love Carmela for my own sake, but for her own, and with that, my torment had ended.

5

Two weeks after these – I hesitate to call them events, for these were huge shifts in my consciousness – I received a letter from Carmela. Would I mind sitting for her, one last time? She wanted to finish my portrait. She said she had wronged me, and wanted to apologize, and give me my picture as a gift.

Compared to the fragile but strengthening joy I felt in my heart, the letter somehow felt redundant. Yet it burned my fingers. It belonged to the old world of sorrowful vales, while I was hovering in the pure ether. Should I abandon my new beloved, beautiful and full of mercy as my own forgiveness had made her, and meet the real Carmela? The idea scared me and I hesitated three or four days before finally overcoming my fears.

The door of her studio, so painfully familiar, was wide open. I quietly walked in. I saw her standing in the depth of the hall. The morning light enveloped her in a halo. She stepped out of this glow and moved towards me. I hadn't seen her for almost a month and was shocked at how she'd changed: her dark complexion concealed neither her paleness nor the bluish circles under her eyes. She looked washed out, pallid; even the well-defined line of her chin seemed weaker. I noticed a shapeless housecoat, so uncharacteristic of her, with an apron stained with paint on top. Apart from these obvious changes there was a more subtle and yet profound transformation: the dry fire that had stormed inside her seemed to be extinguished.

"Sorry, I was painting, didn't have time to change."

I looked at her again and asked if she was all right. She said she had been sick most of the time we hadn't seen each other, but now she had recovered.

She offered me some coffee, and I politely refused: I was in a rush and preferred to get down to our work right away, I told her. She didn't respond, but it was obvious she knew I had nothing planned. We didn't talk while she was painting. Only once were we interrupted, by an unusual whimpering sound coming from the back deck.

A pelican, Carmela explained, with a broken wing, had landed on her deck that morning. She had tried to give it some fresh fish, but it wouldn't touch it. We went out to see the bird: it sat on the floor clumsily, like a duck, tucked in the corner against the glass pane. With its pouch resting on the wooden planks of the deck, it looked quite grotesque. It was all white with a little red rim around the eye that gazed at us with great suspicion. I tried to go closer. The pelican made a clumsy attempt to dash away from me. "Better not touch it," said Carmela. "I tried."

"What's going to happen to it?"

"Most likely, it will die. There is nothing we can do for it."

She went back into the studio. I followed her; she turned around and put her hands on my shoulders.

"I'm so glad you came back," she said, "it was all very foolish, I'm sorry … "

It had been a long time since I'd seen her face so close to mine: no dream or imagination could replace the sensation of holding her in my arms, feeling the warmth of her body.

"I love you," I said, "I never stopped loving you … " She gazed into my eyes, then passed her hand over my cheek. It smelled of paint.

"What answer will you give me then? Have you decided?" She brushed her lips against mine without kissing me, and, slightly bending her knees, she rested her head on my chest.

"Remember? I asked if you'd marry me."

I felt weak in my legs. Of course I remembered, except that the proposition she had made a month ago I had taken as a mockery and an insult.

"Carmela, you don't have to do this to yourself. I know you don't love me. You can't love me. But it doesn't matter, I will always be there for you if you wish. If there is anything you need, just tell me. You don't have to marry me in order to keep me around." My hands started trembling uncontrollably. I wanted to leave. But she prevented me from moving.

"I missed you terribly … " she whispered into my ear and I wasn't even sure that I made out the words correctly. "Terribly, I could barely cope."

"Weren't you with Francisco all this time?"

"I'll explain it to you later, you'll understand, understand it all. I was a fool, forgive me – you do forgive me, don't you?"

"Yes," I said feebly.

"You're the best person I've ever met. They all want me for something: for my eccentric art, or because of the people I know, but none of them love me for me, the way you do. You are a true saint." She started crying. I had never seen her tears before.

"I know we could be happy together. I will be a good wife to you, you'll never regret it. Please, say, *yes*."

I was shattered by her tears and wasn't able to say a word.

"If you love me, please say, *yes*!" The despair in her voice! She did feel guilty after all. And if so, didn't it mean that she loved me after a fashion?

Wild hope surged in my heart:

"Yes," my lips whispered on their own.

"Are you still hesitating? Are you? " She dropped her arms and quickly stepped back. Her eyes were misty.

"No, oh no … I love you. I can't live without you, if that's what …" I drew her back to me.

"I can't live without you either." She wiped the wetness from her eyes.

"Ah, Joe, *corazón*, I'm so tired … Can't even think of painting today." She was now smiling as if relieved of some terrible burden. "Can't we finish your portrait tomorrow? There are so many things I want to do together with you: travel, buy art, entertain interesting people. We will have a happy life, won't we?" She hid her head on my chest, a little girl again.

"Of course, whatever you want, my love … "

On the way back to my hotel, I stopped in bewilderment. What was I doing? One thing was the sublime love dwelling in my soul; quite another was to marry a woman named Carmela. I avoided looking in the direction of that spot on the beach where almost four weeks ago I saw her feeding grapes to Francisco. I knew and trusted my sweet innocent girl. But did I know and trust Carmela? Again I felt that familiar weakness in my legs, that nagging void in my stomach. Remorse apart, it was inconceivable that she would truly want to marry me – that much I understood. What could I offer her? Twice her age, too old to start a family, a foreigner unable to speak her language, knowing not a soul in her country. Could it be my money? She never showed any interest in it, but even if she did, all she needed was to ask. I turned around and retraced my way to the cottage of High Sails. I stood there at the bottom of the stairs for a while, hesitating, listening to the wind. I remembered her tears, the fright in her eyes. How pale she looked, my poor girl, how tired. Didn't I promise to protect her, when we were floating in the ocean of my dream together? And, further, did I want to live, could I

truly live, without her? Now when she said, "I'm yours."
I turned around and went back to my hotel.

6

All my life I've been suffering from migraines that, contrary to what doctors might think, result from the terrible
clutter my undiscriminating memory lumbers upon my
mind: a volley of faces, gestures, scenes I strive to yet can't
erase. The only time my brain gives me respite and my
memory stops collecting its usual crop of disparate im-
pressions is a day or two preceding the onslaught of pain.
In those days my sensations are benumbed. I observe life
as if through the glass of a fish bowl: the luminescent fan
of a tail, the grotesque bulging stare of an underwater
monster swooning by.

I only vaguely remember the kaleidoscope of
Carmela's friends presenting themselves to her apartment
at Chimalistac, a quiet enclave for the well-to-do of Mexico
City, in the days before the wedding: artists, critics,
curators, and socialites. I never got to meet her parents: as
usual they were living in their separate capitals of Europe.
There was a cascade of multi-colored boxes filled with
jewelry, Venetian and Mexican masks, Talavera pottery,
canvases, brushes, shoes, French underwear, embroidered
fabric ordered by Carmela and now arriving to our doors

with a merry-go-round frenzy. I saw myself from the outside: a short bald man wiping sweat off his forehead and writing out checks, then retreating to the coolness of the patio to fill up the glasses of yet another batch of guests.

Strangely, the two images my memory was able to salvage from the murkiness of these prenuptial days had little to do with my marital bliss: one was a huge pyramid assembled of pots of red-and-green leafed poinsettia and posing as a Christmas tree near the Cathedral of Santo Domingo in which we were going to get married; and another, next to that tree, was a nativity crèche with two sheep, an ox and a donkey grazing at the hay in a manger, surrounded by a crude plywood fence. What made these beasts surreal in this anthill city of twenty million is that they were alive. I remember I had a strong desire to stroke the dusty grey curls of the sheep, but then remembered my tuxedo.

My bride's costume à la Frida Kahlo – the multi-layered stiff lace, the intricately embroidered birds of paradise – seemed equally exotic to me; it outshone everything else in the opulent theater production that was my wedding. Carmela's black hair, arranged in triple braids on top of her head and crowned with red roses, her pale solemn face, our kneeling at the altar, our exchanging of the vows and rings, my throwing rice behind my left shoulder to ward off the devil, who, I was told, would always hold his grip, given the slightest chance – all of that is no more than an assemblage of indistinct memories. On stage, I was an uninspired and rather fearful first-timer whom nobody had prepared for his role. The last scene of the show ended with a copious meal. My sense of reality briefly returned to me with the departure of our last guest, a man who vaguely resembled Francisco.

As soon as he closed the door behind him, I went up to Carmela, took her into my arms and planted a long, breathless kiss on her mouth.

She struggled out of my embrace, pushed me away and collapsed on the bed, the gauze of her dress flaring and burying her head. "Leave me alone or I'll scream my lungs out!" Her cry braced my brain with a cement hoop and I descended into pain that lasted for the next three days, obliterating all sensations and memories.

7

Shortly after these events, we went to Canada to settle my inheritance. The morning after our disconcerting nuptial night, my beautiful bride had apologized for her behaviour. The whole "show" had just been too much. Since I had felt much the same, I was mollified. But I was worried about the trip: what would she think about my almost bare apartment at the outskirts of a snowy provincial city?

Of my run-of-the-mill friends, none of whom were artists?

My fears came true: the energy, the sharp purposefulness that Carmela had back home, evaporated; most of the time she just felt bored. Only rarely would she pick up a pencil and sketch the bleak winter landscape that stared at her from behind the window pane: another cement apartment building, two or three cars buried in snow. The climate didn't agree with her, she felt cold and feverish, though I couldn't understand how one could feel both at the same time. Food nauseated her: she found it bland and tasteless.

I noticed the abrupt changes in her mood. She tried to regain the old passion she once, I thought, had for me, but these attempts were so artificial that they left us both greatly embarrassed. After one such bout, she went into a delirium, biting her own fists, beating her hands against the headboard – that wooden, hard, alien sound – and then collapsing with sobs onto the bed. It all horrified me: her violence to herself, her uncontrollable shivering and, worst of all, the way her body would first stiffen, then become soft and listless. I wanted to comfort her, to hold her in my arms, but was afraid to so much as touch her, lest that make her suffering even worse. We were back to the same scene as on the night after our wedding. And I cursed myself for my self-indulgence, for wanting to make love to her incessantly, for believing her when she'd abruptly stop sobbing and jump up shouting "Do it, go ahead, I can't have enough of you!" Then she'd collapse again, all soft and yielding, weeping like a little girl and asking me to forgive her. She'd whisper into my ear that she knew, she understood it all, oh how awful, how very unfair to me, the nicest person on earth, but one day it would be all over, all resolved, for she'd hide in a remote monastery, with daily *Pater Noster,* just like in her Catholic childhood, and could I please bring her some water and kiss her for she needed to calm down. I'd soothe her burning face with a wet towel and then she'd finally fall asleep, felled by fatigue.

It was clear to me that we had to leave Canada, the sooner the better, even if some of the business connected with the inheritance remained unsettled. On a plane back to Mexico, Carmela became sick. We were traveling in business class (was there anything I would begrudge her?) and Carmela didn't mind the skillful care of the flight attendants, but to my "ridiculous doting" she reacted with her usual irritation. I was afraid she'd go into uncontrollable fits again – when she said, her face turned to the window: "Stop fussing. I'm pregnant and if the nausea didn't stop on the ground, you think it would suddenly stop at 15,000 meters?"

The news that I, in my old age, would become a father, threw me into ecstasy! I awkwardly, sheepishly, pulled myself to her side and kissed her hands. She pushed me away. I sat there trying to regain my breath. I didn't mind her dismissals now. I felt this child was God's response to the vows of love and forgiveness that I'd made in the Zipolite hotel before she summoned me to go back to her. Now the three of us – Carmela, me, and the baby – would have a totally different life. I imagined myself appearing arm in arm with her at vernissages and cocktail parties: an older man, with a young beautiful wife bearing his child. The truth is I didn't really know what it was like to have a baby around. All I knew was that the baby girl would make my world brilliantly and freshly new. Somehow I was sure it would be a girl, if only because I would have no use for a boy who, by the mere token of our blood connection, would understand my inner workings, a mirror reflecting my fears, my uncertainties, my pitfalls! The girl, on the other hand, would make me feel real, the way I had never felt before; she would expand my shabby self to new dimensions, for she would be of my flesh, yet as different from me as a remote star.

The only thing I regretted is that my poor darling had not told me about her pregnancy earlier: had I known, I would have seen the tormenting three weeks in Canada in a completely different light. But it was still not too late: I would make up for my previous failures, I'd do anything it took to make her life comfortable, so that she could bring our child into the world without any strain or hardship. I wanted her to remain who she was, a talented and original artist. (I didn't doubt her talent for a moment now! More than that, I was surprised how I could have doubted it in the past.) Yes, we would have a cleaning lady, a cook (Carmela wasn't that keen on cooking), a nanny, and a gardener. She wants to collect art? I'll buy her art. She wanted to try out sculpture and was talking about going to Italy to buy Carrara marble – yes, we would do that too. A hot wave of gratitude was choking me. I got to my feet, and hugging Carmela gently – not to overwhelm her again – went to the end of the passenger cabin, looking for a place where, unwatched, I could give vent to my euphoria.

We bought a run-down villa 100 kilometers from Mexico City. Carmela plunged herself avidly into grand plans of renovations: she redesigned the layout of each room and made drawings for intricate parquet and wallpaper patterns, drapes, and even furniture. In that, as in everything she touched, she never failed to surprise me. I expected her tastes to be cold, sparse, minimalistic. Instead she was seeking to reproduce a Venetian *palaccio* on a smaller scale. She wanted the warm glitter of gilded surfaces; lush silks on the walls in our bedroom; old armchairs, oriental carpets on the marble stairs. She had her mind's eye on authentic Renaissance furniture she hoped to bring back from our travels to Italy that summer.

Carmela was now four months pregnant and we decided not to postpone our trip in spite of the fact that the villa was not finished yet. Before leaving for Italy, we wanted to spend a couple of weeks at the cottage of High Sails, a place I both loved and hated. But Carmela insisted that we go and so we did.

8

How can I conjure up the days that followed? What can do justice to these most horrible – and in hindsight – most idyllic times I've ever had? The delicious tedium of marital bliss (at times I still couldn't believe Carmela was my wife); the sweet lassitude of hot, lazy afternoons. Pregnancy mellowed and pacified her, and her dependency on me I found deeply touching. It seemed that she had finally reconciled with something that was gnarling at her from inside. Our days rolled on from dawn to sunset like identical smooth pebbles; our laziness, our *dolce fare nienti* was complete, permeating the very core of our existence as if some benevolent universal life force was living and breathing for us.

We once spotted a cobweb gently swaying in the air currents between the two potted magnolias in the corner of our bedroom. But to get up with the purpose of ruining the cobweb seemed inconceivable, and so we both stayed put.

After the first three days, we quickly settled into a routine of few words and sparse gestures. I would get up very early and go for a walk along the beach, feeling the cool morning breeze on my face. By the time I returned, Carmela would be still in bed. I'd bring her breakfast and watch her as she poked lazily into the fruit salad that I'd chop up for her. Her face, bloated from sleep and pregnancy, half buried in her hair, darkly contrasted with a white lace nightgown. I found particularly touching all the signs of her condition, everything she herself was unhappy about: her deformed body, the dark spots on her cheeks, her swollen lips and that enigmatic line that stretched along her belly from her navel all the way down to her pubis.

After breakfast, Carmela would paint for two or three hours, moving around with somnambulist slowness. She wanted to be alone then and every time I had to think of a new place to go, of something to do away from the house. She never asked me where I'd gone, or what I'd been doing. I had already explored all the coastal villages and towns; wandered through the dusty streets of Puerto Angel and watched people at Pochutla market. I loved bringing her trinkets from the local artisans: a crudely painted pot, an embroidered napkin, a pair of earrings. She laughed at my unsophisticated taste – and, indeed, I never saw her wearing anything I gave her.

One day it had rained heavily during the night, but let up in the morning, and I wanted to get on a bus early to get groceries at the market. By the time I came back, loaded with fish, cheeses and fruit, it was around ten a.m.

Carmela was not at home and I sat for a while on the deck, looking out at the ocean, and wondering where she was. She must have gone for a quick dip: bathing towel and swimming suit were missing from the drying rack in the bathroom, her nightgown and her house robe scattered over the bed. I felt uneasy about it; we had agreed that she would not go into the ocean alone. But I tried not to be alarmed and made breakfast for the two of us. Then I sat in a rocking chair trying to read a book. Then I went out to the deck again and watched the ocean. Two hours passed and I began to worry in earnest. I went down and walked all the way towards la Playa de l'Amour, the most remote beach separated from our strip by rocks. This was the only gay beach in the country, and affluent yuppies flocked there from Mexico City. I doubted that Carmela would go there but I couldn't spot her anywhere else.

The day was still cloudy, yet you could sense the presence of the hot sun behind the grey puffy veils. I looked at the ocean: its surface had a menacing steel tinge, the breakers higher than usual. I had heard stories of imperceptible whirlpools or underwater currents that pulled even experienced swimmers out into the open sea. By the time they'd realized the danger and shouted for help, it was usually too late; the powerful beat of the surf would muffle any plea for help. Carmela loved swimming and she loved risk. But would she venture alone into the stormy ocean in her condition? I tried to think of other alternatives – perhaps she'd gone to the local bar, or was visiting some friends whom I didn't know? Disturbingly, none of it made any sense.

I went back home, vaguely hoping to find her there. But the house was empty. There was the sound of a tap dripping. I went to tighten it and tripped over a painting leaning against the wall. It was my still-unfinished portrait that Carmela, for some reason, had never wanted to show to me. I don't know what I really expected, but what I saw stunned me.

Instead of a face, the figure on the canvas had a yellow oval, empty inside. In contrast to the oval, my hand (the right hand, to be exact) was painted with meticulous verisimilitude; my veins, dark, bluish ropes, branched under the dried skin in all directions. The left arm was replaced with some protruding form that ended in tree roots, growing through the floor all the way down to the earth, full of dead bodies crunched up like fetuses. I was fingering them with my root-like hand. This is how she sees me, I thought, a faceless monster, a deformity, sorting out corpses.

For the next three days police searched for traces of Carmela. On the third day they found one of her sandals half buried in the sand five miles from our house. Her body, partially decomposed and fed on by sharks, turned up in a rocky bay three weeks later. I refused to see the corpse. It was identified by the wedding ring and by what was left of her swimming suit that they showed to me.

Carmela's friends and fans organized both her funeral mass and her interment. In the church of Santo Domingo, I stood in a semi-dark corner, away from the crowd, nodding silently to the condolences of people passing by. I didn't know the liturgy and watched the priest moving around the closed casket, waving some incense. At one point a tall dark-skinned man came up to me and said he was Carmela's father. Words stuck in my throat and I nodded to him too, without meeting his eyes. Then, closer to the exit, I noticed a kneeling figure. I recognized Francisco. He looked older and somehow smaller than I remembered him. The intensity of his prayer surprised me – I didn't anticipate such religious fervor from this man. He felt my glance, turned around, then quickly withdrew his eyes; I thought I saw tears in them, but perhaps I only imagined them. Something akin to pity stirred in me: after all, he too had loved her. I wanted to talk to him, but then changed my mind. He, however, got off his knees and approached me. "I need to see you," he whispered into my ear. "I have something for you, something belonging to your wife." I said I lived in the villa outside Mexico City in complete seclusion and had no reason to come into town. He replied that he would gladly visit me in the next couple of days and asked for my address.

After Carmela's death, I couldn't see myself staying

either in her studio on the bluffs or in her apartment in Mexico City and so I moved to our unfinished villa. There was no furniture there yet, and I dropped my few possessions right on the floor, away from the mounds of shavings and sawdust gathered in the corner. Some window panes were missing: there must have been break-ins while we were at the coast. A mattress and a blanket served me as a makeshift bed, and this is where I spent day after day in a motionless oblivion, feeling nothing, knowing nothing, coming to my senses only through the involuntary stirrings of my body for they gave me immediate anguish of remembrance, and I whimpered with pain in my delirium. I lost count of days and became only vaguely aware that Francisco hadn't shown up as promised. But what was morning, what was night?

I couldn't sleep at night, and these were the times of my greater lucidity; but the only thing my senses could be alert to was my increasing suffering, and so I hated the nights, their alien dark life, secreting unknown sounds that tormented me with some vague menace. Yet what was there to be afraid of? What kind of loss or pain was there left after Carmela was gone? Once I heard two birds echoing each other: one, with a low forlorn whooping, another with the sharp shriek of a disturbed harlot. I'd never heard anything resembling these sounds, and my soul hung in the interval of anticipation between the shriek and the howl piercing the sticky walls of the night.

By the morning, I started hallucinating and saw Carmela materializing out of these sounds, condensed to the size of an unborn fetus. The fetus needed food, but I had nothing to offer it. Next morning I woke to the ring of the doorbell, which I didn't recognize as such: nobody had ever visited me or rung the bell. I had forgotten all about Francisco, who must have been ringing for quite a while before I opened the door.

He watched me standing in the doorway, a barefoot, feeble old man wrapped in a blanket, my hair messed up from sleep. I couldn't tolerate light by then, and the rays of the sun that Francisco had inadvertently let in blinded me. I observed his tightly fitting black suit, shiny shoes, a silk handkerchief sticking out of his breast pocket. I apologized for my house and my appearance, then began to look for something for us to sit on. Francisco waited silently. I finally fetched two wooden stools, but Francisco remained standing.

"I came to tell you how your wife died. I was there." He fixed his gaze on me.

"My wife drowned in the sea, don't you know?" I said quickly, swallowing a lump of pain.

"She didn't drown on her own. I fed her to the fishes. She was a witch."

"You're raving mad, Francisco. Grief must've made you lose your mind. Please leave. This is a bad time for me to deal with insanity."

"I'm telling you I murdered her. She put a curse on me, so I had to do it," he said, without changing the tone of his voice.

But I saw how pale he grew. His eyes had the glare of a maniac. I became fearful of him and stepped back.

"Wait, I'll call an ambulance – they'll help you ... "

"You'll do no such thing, or you'll go to Hell with her." He quickly stretched his hand towards me. A knife flashed in my eye.

"Your wife agreed to die. I helped her by pushing her off the boat. Virgin Mary showed me the path, blessed be Her Name." He quickly crossed himself. "She came in my dream and said, get a boat. The Virgin Herself stood on the bow and pointed to the place." He crossed himself again. "Carmela went down quickly. A proof she was a witch."

"Did you know she was pregnant with my baby?" I whispered, suddenly having a nightmarish vision of being in front of a murderer, not a raving lunatic.

"Talking of my bastard? It was mine, not yours. His blood on my hands. She told me she was pregnant, I said, ok, then I marry you. She said no, you're poor, I'm going to marry the rich *gringo*."

Still holding his knife in one hand, with the other he pulled two gold watches on long chains out of his breast pocket. He threw them on the stool. One watch slipped off with a clacking sound.

"Take your bloody gold. She kept buying it for me

with your money. I don't need this shit."

I recognized one old watch that had belonged to my father. The other one was new.

"You better strangled your pregnant whore with your own hands, not leave the dirty job for an honest man. She paid with your money for sex with me. Two hundred dollars a fuck. I had to come to your house every morning when you went to the market. But I'm no slave to a whore, I'm a free man!"

"You're a liar, filthy liar!" I protested in a weak, unused voice.

He cocked his head, then dug a letter out of his breast pocket.

"Read this!"

I recognized Carmela's handwriting on a bethumbed, crumpled envelope.

"Can't see without glasses, sorry." My dry throat suddenly made a wimpy, puny sound.

Francisco gave me an odd look, then lowered his eyes and shook his head.

"Go find your glasses, *gringo*, I'll wait."

I hopelessly looked around at the jumble of unsorted things, but was unable to move.

Finally Francisco calmly said, "I'll read it to you."

"*Mi pollo* ... " He stopped and looked at me. "Do you understand Spanish?"

I was dumbfounded.

"I translate," Francisco said in a monotone voice.

"Chicken, why did you refuse to make love to me yesterday? You said it could hurt our baby if mother loves his father's verga."

Do you know *verga?"* Francisco pointed to his crotch. *"If mother loves the father's verga, the baby loves it too. Come tomorrow by ten, when the old fart is at the market. I love watching the sun shining on your butt! His body is cold and wet like worms of death, yours is dry and hot, like the desert. There is no shade in you, only light. I touch you – and I'm on fire. I touch him – and I die. I desire you like no other woman desires you. Forget about marrying this slut of yours: you belong to me alone: your liver, your guts, every hair on your chest … "*

"Enough!" I shouted. "Enough! Get out of here!"

"As you please," said Francisco, stepping back and handing me the letter.

"Before I leave, though, I need five thousand dollars for my wedding. And another five, for the friars at St. Michelle. They'll pray for the soul of my innocent child that I killed."

"I have no money," I said dryly.

"Stop bullshitting, sir," said Francisco, flipping the knife on his hand. "You're a rich man. I need all your cash RIGHT NOW, and a check for the rest of it. After that, get the fuck out of my country!"

I suddenly woke up. "I will call the police, you murderer!"

"I be careful with your words, sir, if I was you," said Francisco. "I already warned you. One more squeak and you're dead. I'll find you don't matter none where." He grabbed me and let me go only after I'd done what he told me to.

Already in the doorway, he turned around:

"As I said, keep your mouth shut, and thank you for your generous gift, sir."

I sat on the floor till the night sprawled over my head all its terrifying magnificence and engulfed the crumpled piece of paper lying next to me.

Carmela, O Carmela! Why didn't you tell me? I would've set you free. I would've let you love the man you loved. I would've raised your child. Once in my dream I promised to follow and protect you wherever you went. Will you ever forgive my betrayal? Will you ever forgive my sordid love that has taken away your life? Will you forgive my old dirty fingers for touching your beatific body? Now in death, your soul is pure again, the way it was when I first saw you: your hair like the wings of the soaring eagle, and your eyes sweet and calm like the sleeping water before it rose and took you away from me forever.

Bird's Milk

The shiny rivets on the edge of the fiber suitcase gleamed under the lamp like lightning bugs about to fly through the irregular spaces between the crocheted snowflakes of the doily covering the lid. The suitcase belonged to the confined rooms of my childhood as solidly as did the old kitchen table which hid under a faded vinyl tablecloth the round dent resulting from my grandparents' years of cracking walnuts with a hammer.

With time, the suitcase itself became furniture: first a TV stand, then a night-table at my grandparents' bed sporting an assortment of disparate objects, most of which had nothing to do with going to bed or getting up: a darning mushroom, a sugar-bin, and a china ballerina on one gilded foot.

"When are they coming? We've run out of sugar," said my grandmother, inspecting the empty bowl on top of the suitcase. "You know Liza has a sweet tooth."

"Won't hurt them if they use sliced apples instead," said my grandfather. A severe diabetic, he had no use for sugar and was convinced that his own strange tea drinking ritual would suit everybody just fine.

My grandparents would fall into prolonged silences interrupted only by the sound of a spoon rattling in a glass.

My grandfather never drank tea out of cups but preferred a glass in a simple metal holder. Why he needed to stir slices of apple into his tea was a mystery to me: perhaps he liked to watch them whirl in the water, a little chasing game he created; or perhaps, the chime of the spoon reminded him of the morning tea trays rattling glass on metal, on the long distance trains when he was the Chief Railways Inspector before the war.

The Levins, visiting my grandparents, were an elderly couple, always dressed in dark baggy coats. They would remove the galoshes from their felt boots and put them side by side – one pair small, another big – in the hallway, leaving two muddy puddles of melting snow on a threadbare mat. The knock of their knuckles on my grandparents' door was purely symbolic: hardly a sound at all. The Levins sat never changing their postures, and no chairs ever cracked under their weightlessness. They were strangely quiet, these two guests. Auntie Liza, with her prominent Jewish nose and heavy half-closed eyelids, resembled a small tired bird. It was impossible to imagine this woman ever being young or vivacious. Her husband, whom everybody, including his wife, called simply Levin, was tall and emaciated, with a mass of black hair that sharply contrasted with his crumpled face and pale lifeless lips. Levin rarely spoke, but when he did it was always in the same monotone:

"Joseph, if Vladimir goes to Minsk to get the papers,

I'll wait in Moscow till he returns. You know it's my last chance."

"Where are you going to stay in the meantime?" said my grandfather.

"Why do you ask?" grumbled my grandmother. "They have no place, you know that!" She looked hesitatingly around the room. "They could stay with us while waiting," she said in a quieter tone.

"Oh no, we won't inconvenience you," said Aunt Liza, her eyes downcast. "Levin has already got six orders from Ryazan. I'm sure there will be more, once we arrive and people hear about us. We were planning to leave tomorrow."

"Going without a passport? Ryazan is not a small place."

"I'm telling Levin, small villages are much better: out of sight, out of mind. But he won't listen to me," said Aunt Liza without lifting her eyes.

"I'll take a risk, it's only three or four days, right? I'll make a good buck and pay Gromov for the passport," said Levin.

"I wouldn't count on three days. It can be a week, two weeks, you never know. As for Vladimir … you know my son. He doesn't always knock at the right door. I can't go … people might recognize me …" said my grandfather and stirred his tea again.

"You? Well, that's out of the question, Joseph, that's

understood." Levin sighed. "But I don't want to put your son at risk either, not on my account. Though I think it's safe. I was told by people I trust."

"You think so? If I believed that, I would myself urge my son to go. What if it's a trap?"

"Look," said Levin. "Gromov knows the guy. He is Aaron's relative, completely reliable."

"And where is Aaron?" asked my grandfather, moving his glass away and putting both hands on the table. "You tell me, where is Aaron?" He pointed to the suitcase in the corner. "This has been waiting for him for eight years."

"He will return," said Levin quietly. "You'll see. But you should have opened the suitcase and looked inside."

"If he is returning, why would I open it? It's your brother's. You should take it."

"Where would I put it, Joseph? I have no home. Besides, it was entrusted to you. You should keep it till he returns."

My grandfather bent towards Levin:

"He will not return. Don't fool yourself."

There was silence.

"There is a difference between fooling oneself and having hope," said Levin finally. "Without hope, where would I be now, Joseph?"

Again there was a pause. My grandmother brought out two more glasses in metal sleeves. She put a plain saucer with a small heap of round crackers on the table. Then she poured pale tea into both glasses. Auntie Liza took one cracker, soaked it in her tea, and bit on it with her few remaining front teeth. Levin held the glass without drinking, warming his transparent fingers with its heat. I was afraid to look at his mutilated right hand. His thumb and an index finger were missing.

It was only recently that the Levins found each other after twelve years of labor camps. In 1936, Levin, a biologist and the director of a research institute, had confessed that he was a paid Trotskyite agent, a tool of the American intelligence services assigned to drown the conquests of the Socialist Revolution in its own blood by growing a deadly virus in his institute's lab. The virus killed 1470 horses, 3304 pigs, and 1900 cows in one district alone. His wife Liza confessed that, as her husband's accomplice, she dreamt up a "smoke tax" and personally collected it from all the peasants who had chimneys in the nearby villages to finance the subversive activities of her man.

Miraculously, the Levins had survived the camps: Levin felling trees in Solovki, 150 kilometers off the Arctic Circle, and Liza in Siberia, half a continent away, near Turukhansk. Liza turned out to be a fine calligrapher and painter, and instead of building the Salekhard railway road – the "Death Road" as women in the camp nicknamed it – she painted murals for the "Red Corners," the official rooms outfitted with Lenin's busts and red banners. She also designed *Lightnings,* the Gulag propaganda bulletins.

The two beat the odds again when they reunited – only to discover that the miracle of their reunion was marred: their son Leonid was nowhere to be found.

The day after his parents' arrest, men in civilian clothes took the five-year-old into an orphanage, where both his first and last name were changed. That was, no doubt, the manifestation of justice but also mercy, aimed at removing the shameful stains from the boy's biography by the simple act of severing any links with his parents, the accursed enemies of the people. As Comrade Stalin had pointed out, no son should be held responsible for the crimes of his father.

When all their efforts to find Leonid led to nothing, Auntie Liza gently but firmly slipped into another world. She would tilt her bird's head to one side listening intently to God's divine lisp, which she alone could discern. Aunt Liza never questioned God's benevolent intercession into her family's affairs: it was only a question of time, and of all people, Liza knew everything there was to know about time. She also knew that God, in His infinite mercy, after munching some sounds in His ancient mouth, would dictate to her the initial letter, then the first and the second syllables of her child's assumed name, and finally, reveal all: first, patronymic, and the last name. None of it would be as sweet as the boy's real name: "Leonid Lvovich Levin." No, it would be a rough name, in itself a guarantor of its bearer's survival. Something like Boris Petrovich Stepin, or Petr Andreevich Drozdov, a name with sharp corners, more palatable in this world.

The moment would always come when Aunt Liza would quietly move her tea glass to the side, get a pencil stub out of her purse and make some quick notes in her elegant tiny writing on a scrap of paper buried somewhere in the old bag. She anticipated the revelation of the secret with humility, that moment when she'd see the name appear on paper, the right one, and then fill her mouth with its new sounds, savor them, sing them quietly to herself, and finally carry them to the Central Information Bureau in her open palm, so that in a month, at most two or three, her little boy now grown up, still pale and scraggy but all right, would run into her arms out of piles of stamped and signed papers, the jumble of metal orphanage beds, lice-infested shaven heads, steel mugs and plates, railway stations guarded with dogs, forlorn locomotive hoots, abandoned construction sites, entangled wire, fallen electrical poles, frozen dirt, coal piles soiling virgin snow across the immeasurable indifferent white expanses of her land: "Mama, *mamoshka,* I'm here! I knew you would find me!"

"Sonia," my grandfather turned to me. "Go out and play. Go."

"Leave her alone. Where will the child go? It's late," said my grandmother and closed the curtains.

"Come, come over here, then," my grandfather

motioned. "What's today, Sonia, Monday? Check if the candies in my pocket grew all right. Give me your hand, right there, see? Now, which one you want? A Bear in the North or a Golden Rooster?"

"Bird's Milk," I said firmly. "I want Bird's Milk."

"No, that one doesn't grow on Mondays ..."

"Tuesdays, then?"

"I'm afraid not."

"How about Thursdays?"

"Well ... maybe this Friday."

"Ah, you're cheating! Candies don't grow in the pockets. You buy them in the store."

"Who told you that? Have you ever seen any candies in the store?"

My grandfather was right. In 1948, there were no candies or apples to be bought, but as a former secretary of the regional party committee and a War Hero, he was entitled to a special food ration from the party's internal food distribution centre.

"Look," said my grandfather, "Here is the Bear in the North. Did you see it yesterday? No. So what happened overnight? It just grew ..." He pointed to his pocket again.

"I want Bird's Milk."

"But birds don't make milk, didn't you know?"

"If you say candies grow in your pocket, then birds make milk too. And besides, I just had Bird's Milk yesterday. They are the best candies in the world!"

"Where did you get them?" asked Aunt Liza, who suddenly awakened from her trance. She scooped the scraps of paper into her purse and gazed into my face.

"Tanya gave me," I said innocently.

"Tanya …who is Tanya? And where did Tanya get them from?" Aunt Liza's eyes seemed alight. "Up North that's what I craved for most, candies …"

"Her father brings Bird's Milk from work," I said quietly, looking away.

Years later, I found out that Tanya's father was a prosecutor at Lubyanka. He called Lubyanka "the organs."

I felt guilty having tasted Bird's Milk while Aunt Liza had not and now wanted it as badly as a little girl would.

"Aren't there lots and lots of candies, up North, Aunt Liza?" I asked, "Don't Bears from the North live there?"

"No, my sweetheart, there were no candies at all. But what does Bird's Milk taste like, tell me?"

"Like … like … like chocolate waffles."

"Chocolate waffles …" Aunt Liza repeated the words and looked away. She turned back to me. "If Tanya ever gives you another candy, will you treat me to one?"

"I promise. When I grow up and earn a lot of money, I shall buy you a whole box of Bird's Milk!" I felt sorry for Aunt Liza. Her eyelids looked so heavy. I wanted to hold them open with my fingers.

"Joseph, let's open Aaron's suitcase, and see what's inside," said her husband Levin. "Maybe there are some papers, or some clothing Vladimir can use if he goes to Minsk."

"Now go and play with your dolls, Sonia," said my grandfather.

"I don't want dolls. I want to see what's in the suitcase," I said.

Without the doily, the suitcase looked naked, ominous as if a stranger had suddenly appeared in the room. It wasn't new. Cuts and scars traced diagonals across its surface. My grandfather pressed hard on the metal buttons. The two clasps popped up and the lid fell open. The women held their breath. On the top lay yellowed newspapers with washed-out print in an unfamiliar script. My grandfather removed the newspaper. I could smell tobacco and a faint odor of *eau-de-cologne*. We all stared at the clothes: canvas tennis shoes, striped, foreign-looking shirts, a belt with a bright-gold buckle, turtleneck sweaters the likes of which none of us had ever seen. None of it seemed to interest my grandfather at all. He rummaged. He was looking for papers about the fate of his vanished friend Aaron Levin.

There were none; instead, from underneath the heap of clothes a piece of fabric emerged, a print, shimmering tiny pink and purple flowers on a pale-blue meadow. It was a woman's scarf that must have somehow lost its way on the road of war before finding its unlikely shelter. My grandmother admiringly stroked the scarf, then handed it to Aunt Liza who examined it against the light and then pressed it to her face with small whimpering sounds.

But the scarf was only a prelude. My grandfather's excavation had unearthed the edge of a photograph at the bottom of the suitcase. I wondered as we pulled it out whether the young woman owned the scarf. It was an exotic, not Russian face, framed with thick black curls. The face of a beauty. She wasn't smiling but her dark eyes were all sparks. Her lips were parted slightly with a hint of mischief as if she was gazing at a marvel no one else saw.

"I didn't know he had a woman in Spain …" said my grandfather, examining the picture.

"Aaron's fiancée," replied Levin. "They met in 1939 in Barcelona, shortly before it fell to the Nationalists. He was going to bring her to Moscow and marry her here."

My grandfather looked at Levin and said nothing. Then, in reverse order, he started putting clothing back in the suitcase: the photograph on the bottom, sweaters, shirts, tennis shoes, and finally, the newspaper. He locked the suitcase and carried it back to the bed.

"Yes," he said after a pause, "I hope Aaron will return."

Aaron was born to a Jewish family in Lithuania. Together with his elder brother Lev Levin, he came to Moscow to make the Revolution. That's where the two brothers met my grandfather, then an aspiring Komsomol leader. The three friends became inseparable. But the Revolution was soon over, replaced by the Civil War. "All men are Brothers! Down with the Rotting Corpse of the Bourgeoisie! Labor will Rule the World!"

These were exciting times. You could feel the air crackling with euphoria. Aaron was good with horses, and with his saber in hand he galloped from the Western to the Eastern Fronts, cleansing capitalist filth from the world, protecting the oppressed, summarily executing the enemy, all in the name of Comrade Lenin, the World Revolution and the International Proletariat. But then the Civil War came to an end, leaving in its wake the Heroic Collectivization, Heroic First Five-Year Plan, Heroic Construction of the First Metropolitan in the world, Heroic Conquest of the Arctic, Heroic Stakhanovism Movement, Heroic Three-Months-on-the-Ice-Floe-from-Pacific-to-Antarctic-without-Food, Heroic Soviet-Woman-the-Mother-of-Ten-Winner-of-Parachute-Jumping-Tournament. Aaron yearned for another revolution. He found it in Spain's International Brigades. When the Republic failed, he fled back to Russia, stopping at my grandfather's. He was trying to arrange the papers to get his fiancée across the border. One sunny morning he went to the post-office to send her a telegram. Nobody saw him again.

"Now at least we know what's in the suitcase," said Levin. "You keep it, Joseph. Keep it."

"I will," said my grandfather. "But I won't send my son to Minsk, Levin. This is a frame-up, don't you see?

You have only a 'wolf's' passport, that's true. You can't live in Moscow, or in any other city, but at least you're alive ..."

"Alive! You call this a life?" my grandmother interrupted. "Nobody would even register them! They tried Tver, they tried Ryazan, they tried every damn pin on the map. No place, nobody would have them!"

"Don't you worry, Anna," said Liza. She seemed to be looking sideways, her gaze avoiding the others. "People are kind. They give us everything we need: food, shelter, a place to keep our equipment. Sometimes money too."

Many years later, I recalled Liza's words. In the 1960s, when nobody sitting around that table in that remote, dimly lit room was alive, I discovered why people had been kind to the Levins.

After twelve years in the camps, denied residence and the right to work, the two of them once again found a way to hoodwink fate. For several years after the war they walked from village to village, magnifying passport-size photographs of the dead. The pattern was always the same: suspicions when they arrived and grateful farewells when they left. In many places after the war, the names of the dead outnumbered the living and the Levins never lacked for work. Levin learned that it was easier to look into the eyes of the dead on a piece of a photo paper than into the eyes of their widows and mothers as they opened the door to ask what was it he wanted from them.

Levin proved to be very good at his new trade. The men on the tiny photographs he was given were stern, solemnly closed into themselves, with a generic, vacant expression. But when he enlarged and retouched them, they acquired a benevolent, soft, even mildly romantic look. Under Levin's skillful hands, these slightly out-of-focus, vague faces would come to peace with their destiny. Mounted on the wall, or placed on a chest of drawers next to a small cluster of artificial flowers, they finally achieved immortality. At long last, safety was theirs.

The Levins were doing so well that they even managed to put away some money, the investment in the elusive dream of their future freedom.

My grandfather was as good as his word: he kept his son from travelling to Minsk. It must have been the old man's sixth sense, his insider's knowledge of the manhunter's lore that saved my father's life. But it didn't save Levin's. He was arrested again, charged this time with poisoning the wells in a city he'd never visited. Levin died in a labor camp the year before Stalin's death.

What happened to his brother's suitcase? It had somehow disappeared from our family orbit. I vaguely remember my grandfather wearing colorful turtlenecks and gaudy short-sleeved shirts that looked strange on this taciturn and somber man.

After Levin's arrest, Auntie Liza went into hiding.

A moving target, she rode the freights, slept in railway station latrines, shipping containers, or abandoned sheds. The blind chance that had destroyed her son and husband at the end let Liza off the hook. When I saw her again in much milder, 'vegetarian' times she was toothless, all skin and bones, her hair gone completely white; more than ever she seemed to belong to the weightless feathered tribe, the only one that could go where it pleased in her homeland.

I visited her in her six-square-meter 'corner' in a communal apartment shared by eight families. There was almost no furniture in her room. Aunt Liza sat at the window looking vacantly into the street. Since her husband's death, she had loads of time on her hands: she wasn't scribbling names on scraps of paper any longer. God had forsaken this land – she now knew it.

In late May of 1964, Auntie Liza received a summons. As a victim of Stalin's 'purges' she was now entitled to her own apartment, a small second-floor studio with a separate kitchenette and a bathroom. Coincidentally, she was supposed to view it on her 65th birthday. To our surprise, Aunt Liza refused to even look at the new place, never mind move in. It was then that my brother Sergey and I came up with a plan. We bought a big bouquet of flowers, a biscuit cake, a box of marshmallows and even a bottle of champagne, intending to invite all Liza's neighbors to her birthday party. But first, we wanted to talk her into getting into Sergey's new car for a thirty-minute drive to her new apartment. How exciting! The first housing projects in twenty years since the war! Fresh air, sunshine! Young mothers strolling with their prams!

"The second floor would be perfect, just perfect for you!" I kept saying. "The first is unsafe because of breaks-in; the third, too high without an elevator, but the second? It is really the luck of the draw!"

"You'll have your own bathroom, too!" my brother egged Liza on. "When was the last time you had your own tub with running water? Your own kitchen? Never, right?" Aunt Liza raised her eyes to Sergey but said nothing. I started setting the table for the guests who would be there when we returned. Then I opened a box of chocolate and handed it over to Aunt Liza. "Have some," I said, "before we go ..."

She was hesitant and looked away.

"Please take some," I repeated. Aunt Liza looked at me and her face suddenly brightened up.

"Do you remember?" she said. Her fingers took tentative aim at one accordion-pleated pink rosette. "Right after the war, you were eight or nine then, and you promised when you grew up,to buy me a whole box of Bird's Milk?"

"Come on, let's go, Aunt Liza," said my brother impatiently. "We'll take the marshmallows with us. You can eat all you want on the way there ..."

The new apartment smelled of paint and thinner. Newspapers were scattered on the floor bordered by piles of plaster in the corners. We propped Aunt Liza on a stool, the only chair left by the construction workers in the middle of an empty room.

In the kitchen the pipes under the sink were sloppily connected. Water dripped onto the floor. While Sergey was looking for a bucket, I looked out the kitchen window. Construction leftovers littered the landscape, competing with tree stumps and mud puddles dotting the bare earth. But one bush of white lilac survived, overlooked by the bulldozers. It stood alone, intact, tall and in full bloom. I tugged at the window: I needed some fresh air and I wanted to let the scent of lilac into the flat. "Aunt Liza! Look what we found!" I wanted her to see the bush and tugged again. The window was painted shut. Sergey found a knife, poked here and there. Just when the window seemed to yield we heard a thud and a weak cry. In the living room Aunt Liza lay on the floor next to the stool. Her hands clutched her chest and she gasped in whistling gulps.

There was no telephone in the apartment. Sergey ran outside to look for the public phone. I sat on the floor next to Aunt Liza, helplessly watching her jerk her head from side to side. Beneath her face, beads of sweat collected on the floor. She was still alive when they carried her through the narrow door, twisting the stretcher awkwardly.

It was in the ambulance that God, who Liza believed had abandoned her forever, finally returned to her side, gently took her by the hand and led her into the golden glow of spring. She floated free on the fragrance of lilacs above her longed-for city, over the young girls in school uniform skirts playing hopscotch on the asphalt, over crowds still in winter coats queueing for food in great dark zigzag lines; over the streetcars cutting quick arpeggios on their celestial cords, smudging every turn with sheaves of fire. By the time the ambulance stopped in front of the Corinthian columns of the Central Hospital, Aunt Liza had already joined her husband and son. She joined them in that radiant, shimmering land that alone had given her a shelter and a permanent home, a land of honey and Bird's Milk, the land she would never need to escape.

LaVergne, TN USA
16 August 2009
154933LV00002B/3/P